The Catbird Caper

THE
CATBIRD
CAPER

Kristin Eckhardt

Guideposts Books
CARMEL, NEW YORK

www.guideposts.org
(800) 431-2344
Guideposts Books & Inspirational Media Division

Cover and interior design by Cindy LaBreacht
Cover art by Gail W. Guth
Map by Jim Haynes, represented by Creative Freelancers, Inc.
Typeset by Nancy Tardi
Printed in the United States of America

For my cousin Angela Schacht,
a wonderful person and an excellent service dog trainer,
and in memory of my great-grandmother
Viola DuFrane Heim.

To U.S.A.

ORCAS

LUMMI

N
W   E
S

CYPRESS

GUEMES

To ANACORTES

FIDALGO ISLAND

*SPARROW ISLAND IS FICTITIOUS

CHAPTER ✿ ONE

ABBY STANTON HOPED she wasn't forgetting something important.

She stood in the laboratory of the Sparrow Island Nature Conservatory on Sunday afternoon, mentally reviewing her list. As the Associate Curator, she performed many duties and wanted to make sure they were all covered before she left on her trip the next day.

"Look at that," Bobby McDonald said, pointing to the tiny bird in the cage next to him. "He's finally eating something."

Her ten-year-old neighbor often helped out at the conservatory and he especially liked assisting her in the lab. He had a quick mind and a cheerful demeanor that made him a pleasure to have around.

Abby moved in for a closer look at the orphaned owlet. She'd found him two days ago, abandoned near a nest that had been ravaged by a predator. The owlet had been dehydrated and listless, but now looked much more lively since he'd been given food and water.

As an ornithologist and wildlife rehabilitator, Abby knew that good nutrition and hydration were half the battle in preparing her patients to return to the wild.

"Will you check on him for me while I'm gone?" Abby asked Bobby.

"Sure," he replied, "I'll stop by every day after school."

"If there are any problems, just give me a call on my cell phone or at the Bristol Hotel in Seattle."

"We'll be fine," Bobby assured her, hunching down in front of the cage so he was eye to eye with the owlet. "Won't we, Fred?"

"Fred?" Abby echoed.

Bobby grinned up at her. "That's his name. Don't you think it fits him?"

Abby laughed, a pang of homesickness hitting her when she realized she'd be away from the job she loved for an entire week. Yet, she couldn't pass up this opportunity to participate in one of the few television shows that she enjoyed.

Antique Adventures was coming to film in Seattle and Abby, along with her older sister Mary and a small contingent of Sparrow Island residents, was planning to attend. Each of them was taking along an antique for appraisal by the show's experts. Hugo Baron, Abby's boss and the Curator of the conservatory, still hadn't revealed to Abby which of his many treasures he intended to bring.

The group had all reserved rooms at the Bristol Hotel and planned to depart from Friday Harbor on San Juan Island tomorrow morning aboard the *Victoria Clipper*. Since both Hugo and Abby would be absent for the week, Hugo had contacted Cecil Adams, a naturalist and good friend, to keep watch over the conservatory until they returned.

"You and Fred have a good time while I'm gone," Abby told Bobby, taking one last look around the lab. She'd been preparing for this trip for several weeks, but still kept finding last-minute things to do.

"Oh, we will," Bobby promised. "I'll keep his cage clean and make sure he has plenty to eat and drink. I've even hooted at him a few times to teach him how to do it, but he just looks at me like I'm crazy."

"Fred will hoot soon enough," Abby assured him. "That's a natural instinct for an owl." She was more worried about the owlet learning to hunt and care for himself in the wild. But she'd tackle that problem when she returned from her trip.

Fortunately, Fred was the only animal in the laboratory. She'd recently released a red fox back into the wild after a long recovery. It would have been much more difficult to leave if the lab had been full of injured animals that needed her care.

"What are you taking to the show?" Bobby asked her. Despite his youth, he enjoyed the interesting stories on *Antique Adventures* and was excited by the possibility that Abby might appear on television.

"The bird painting that I found at a flea market on San Juan Island," Abby told him. "I love the painting and the seller told me it might be a John James Audubon."

"Who's that?"

"He was a wildlife artist who lived during the early 1800s. His life-sized bird paintings are quite famous. There are over four hundred of them in a book called *Birds of America*. I have a copy of it in my office if you ever want to borrow it."

"Cool," Bobby replied. "So your bird painting might be worth a lot of money?"

Abby smiled. "Well, I only paid ten dollars for it at the flea market, so I doubt it. Since I like the painting so much I got a good bargain no matter what."

"I hope you get on television," Bobby said as they left the laboratory.

The Sparrow Island Nature Conservatory comprised several acres on the east coast of Sparrow Island. Abundant with birds and wildlife, the conservatory also featured an onsite natural history museum and an observation platform.

Abby wasn't quite as excited at the prospect of appearing on television as Bobby. Her primary interest in attending the show was to get the bird painting evaluated and appraised. However, she and her sister Mary had gone shopping for clothes earlier in the week just in case they found themselves in front of a television camera.

"I'll check on Fred tomorrow," Bobby promised her, backing toward his mom's car waiting outside. "Have a good trip!"

"Thank you, Bobby."

Abby headed toward The Nature Museum, a two-story building made of stucco and stone that featured various wildlife exhibits. She checked her watch as she walked to her office, not wanting to be late for supper at the Stanton farm. Her mother had extended the invitation after church this morning, her manner making Abby suspect this visit might entail more than eating.

Whatever the agenda, she looked forward to spending the time with her parents. Mary and her beau, Deputy Sheriff Henry Cobb, were attending a flower show on Orcas Island and wouldn't be back in time to join them. Though Mary had retired from full-time work at her flower shop, Island Blooms, she still couldn't resist checking out the competition.

Abby flipped on the light in her office, her gaze landing on the bird painting that leaned against the wall. She'd been storing it there, not certain where to hang it. Even if it didn't turn out to be an original Audubon, Abby was enchanted by the painting and eager to find out more about its origin.

Moving closer to the painting, she studied the fine brush strokes of the detailed feathers over the breast of the gray catbird. A few small water stains marred the bottom corner of the canvas, but otherwise the painting was in excellent condition.

It was unsigned, which added to the mystery. She'd heard rumors that John J. Audubon had given away several of his bird drawings in the early years of his career and she wondered if this could be one of them. The possibility intrigued her since Abby had always loved mysteries.

She carefully picked up the painting and carried it over to her desk to wrap it in brown paper. Once that was done, she consulted her list, surprised to find that she had nothing left to do.

"I guess I'm all set," she said aloud.

Taking one last look around her office, Abby breathed a sigh of relief. She loved her job, but she'd learned during her years of teaching at Cornell that a vacation always refreshed and revitalized her.

Rev. Hale often spoke of the importance of refilling the spiritual well with rest and meditation. Abby liked to apply those same principles to her career and believed this trip was just what she needed to renew her professional vigor.

CHAPTER ❧ TWO

A THRONG OF WHITE AND yellow daisies greeted Abby as she pulled into the long driveway that led to Stanton Farm. Situated on the east coast of Sparrow Island, the farm's rich soil provided sustenance to the organic vegetable crops her parents produced for sale. Long, lush rows of blue huckleberry bushes and rugosa roses bordered the farmyard.

As she got out of her car, Abby inhaled a hint of lavender in the September air from the pick-your-own crop that delighted so many tourists during the annual Lavender Festival.

"I'm up here," Ellen Stanton called from the open attic window.

Abby waved up to her mother, then headed for the house. She walked through the back screen door and into the kitchen. A pot of coffee was brewing on the counter, the comforting aroma mingling with the savory scent of a roast baking in the oven. Abby knew her father and their beloved hired man Sam Arbogast would be in soon for supper, so she hurried upstairs to find her mother.

As she headed upstairs, the familiar creak of the stairs reminded Abby of all the times she and her sister had raced up these same wooden steps, anxious to hear their father read them a bedtime story. He always read a parable from the Bible using simple language a child could understand and interspersing those timeless stories with his humor and love and patience.

Mary could no longer climb these stairs, since she had become paralyzed from a car accident. The Stanton home had been made as accessible as possible for her sister's wheelchair, but the narrow stairway leading up to the second floor bedrooms couldn't be renovated due to the construction of the old house. Abby realized how often she took things for granted, like climbing stairs, and how such a simple act could provoke such precious memories.

"Thank you, Lord," she prayed quietly when she reached the top floor, "for the gifts that surround us every day. Open my eyes that I may see them all."

"Abby?" Ellen called from above her.

Abby walked over to the old pull-down ladder that hung suspended in the middle of the hallway. She peered up into the dark, square opening in the tiled ceiling. "I'm coming up now, Mom."

"All right, dear. Be careful."

She couldn't remember how many years it had been since she'd climbed the ladder that led to the attic. Now, as she ascended the narrow rungs, Abby wondered if it was safe for her mother to make this journey. It would be all too easy for Ellen to slip and fall at her age.

Walking into the attic was like entering another world.

The dormers added quaint angles to the large room and the sun cast a hazy, golden glow through the tiny window on the south wall.

Abby and Mary used to play up here as children, using the attic as a perfect stage to create a desert island or an isolated mountaintop retreat or whatever exotic locale their imaginations could conceive.

"Mom?" Abby called out, her eyes adjusting to the shadows. "I'm over here."

Abby sneezed at the dust hovering in the air, then turned to see her mother seated in a far corner under the rafters.

The attic was piled high with keepsakes and old furniture. As she passed one of the open boxes, Abby saw her old high school yearbook on top of the pile. Unable to resist, she reached down and picked it up, smoothing one hand over the faded gilt letters on the navy blue cover.

She opened it up, smiling at the photographs of her old classmates. Their clothing and hairstyles marked them as children of the sixties. There was a picture of her wearing a pair of bright, flowered bell-bottom pants that made Abby laugh out loud.

"I can't believe you let me out of the house in this outfit," Abby said, turning the yearbook around to show the picture to her mother.

Ellen smiled. "As I remember it, those pants were your favorite birthday present that year. You got angry at Mary when she wore them out on a date and hid them in your room after that."

Abby shook her head at the memory, wondering how such a thing as a pair of pants could be so important to her. Time had a way of winnowing out the wheat from the chaff in life.

Those teenage years were far behind her. At fifty-five, she now preferred comfort over style.

Abby fielded the obstacle course of boxes and other debris to reach her mother's side. "What are you doing up here?"

Ellen sighed. "I debated whether to even dig it out after all these years, but I know you and your sister are leaving for the *Antique Adventures* show tomorrow and I couldn't resist." She held up an old gold locket. "Do you remember this?"

Abby reached out to cradle the small oval locket in the palm of her hand. She hadn't seen it for decades, but knew it contained a tiny wisp of faded red hair inside. "Grandma Lora's locket."

Ellen nodded, her eyes misting at the memory of her mother. "Mama never took it off."

Abby remembered. Grandma Lora had never worn any other jewelry, only the locket and her plain gold wedding band. Her simple way of life and kind, generous heart had made her a favorite of the Stanton girls. Even after all these years, just the aroma of gingerbread could bring all those wonderful memories flooding back.

Yet, despite Grandma Lora's love for her family, there was one thing she'd always refused to talk about—her childhood. Born in New York City, she'd become an orphan at the age of eleven. Abby's research into that time period had revealed that it was not unusual for orphans to be disparaged and thought of as second-class citizens. Perhaps that was the reason for Grandma Lora's silence on the subject.

"I miss her so," Ellen said. "After she passed away, it hurt me too much to look at this locket, so I put it away up here with the rest of her belongings."

Abby wrapped her arms around her mother, knowing the

locket brought her both pleasure and pain. The memories were bittersweet with so many unanswered questions about Grandma Lora's past.

"This locket," Ellen continued, "was the only thing she brought with her on the orphan train, other than the few secondhand clothes she owned." She sighed. "I just wish I knew why it meant so much to her and whose lock of hair she kept inside of it."

"She never told you either?" Abby knelt down beside her mother, remembering all the times she and Mary had pestered their grandmother for the story behind the locket she wore.

Ellen shook her head. "I eventually learned to stop asking her about it. Mama never liked to talk about her past—especially her years as an orphan. She said God always took good care of her, blessing her with a new family when she stepped off that orphan train in Nebraska."

Her grandmother's reluctance to talk about those experiences had always intrigued Abby. She'd read books about the orphan trains that used to run between the East Coast and the Midwest from the mid-nineteenth century to the early twentieth century.

A young minister by the name of Charles Loring Brace had been startled by the street children he'd seen running in gangs when he moved to New York City. So he'd started the Children's Aid Society and fostered the idea of sending these orphaned and neglected children to Midwest farm families to be adopted.

Abby shuddered to think of the crude selection process. An orphan train stopped at each small town along the way, then the children were led out onto the train platform or a small stage. Townspeople and farmers hoping to adopt could pick a child out of the crowd. Sometimes siblings were separated and never saw each other again.

There was little oversight back then to make sure the new parents were fit to take care of a child. Fortunately for Grandma Lora, she'd been taken in by a kind family that didn't abuse her or treat her like an unpaid servant. Other children hadn't fared as well.

Grandma Lora's faith had been forged in those hard, early years and never wavered. Abby couldn't think of a better legacy for the woman to pass onto her children and grandchildren.

"Will you take this with you and see what you can find out about it?" Ellen asked, placing the locket in Abby's palm. "I don't really care about an appraisal. This is priceless to me, whatever its monetary value. I just want to find out something . . . *anything* . . . about it."

The locket was warm from her mother's hand. Abby curled her fingers around it, a lump in her throat. "Of course I will."

Ellen gave her a watery smile. "Thank you, Abby. Even if all we discover is where the locket came from, we might be able to find out something about your grandmother's early years before she arrived in Nebraska. I know it's a long shot . . ."

Abby tucked the locket safely inside her pocket. "It will be worth it, no matter what happens. And I promise to take good care of it."

Ellen patted her arm. "I know you will." Then she rose stiffly to her feet. "I'd better finish getting supper ready. It's getting late."

"May I help?"

"You can snap some beans for me if you'd like."

Abby couldn't think of anything she'd rather do than indulge in the comfort of snapping beans at the kitchen table just as she'd done as a child—a child who had grown up snug and secure in her parents' loving home.

As she followed her mother downstairs she found herself wondering about another child. Her Grandma Lora had been all alone in the world when she'd boarded the orphan train that would lead her to a new state and a new family and a new life.

A Bible verse echoed in Abby's head—the same one Grandma Lora had often recited.

"You are my hiding place; you will protect me from trouble and surround me with songs of deliverance" (Psalm 32:7).

Perhaps that verse had sustained Grandma Lora on her long, fateful journey. Abby would never know.

The locket was the only key to Grandma Lora's past. She hoped the jewelry experts at *Antique Adventures* could tell her something about it. Maybe discovering the history and origin of the locket would finally give her mother—and herself—some answers after all these years.

CHAPTER ❧ THREE

THE NEXT MORNING, ABBY washed the breakfast dishes while she waited for Mary to return from Island Blooms. Her sister had received an urgent telephone call from the manager, Candace Grover, asking for assistance. So Mary had made a quick trip to the shop while Abby finished packing.

Wiping her hands on a dishtowel, Abby glanced up at the clock. If Mary didn't get here soon, they'd miss the ferry that would take them to San Juan Island to board the *Victoria Clipper.*

Picking up the telephone, Abby dialed her sister's cell phone. It rang four times, then went to voicemail, so she left a message. "Hey, Mary, it's me. We need to be at the dock in twenty minutes, so I hope you're on your way home. See you soon."

Abby hung up the phone, hoping her sister was already on her way. Mary had been looking forward to this trip as much as Abby. *Antique Adventures* was Mary's favorite television show, and she had a special heirloom from her deceased husband Jacob that she wanted appraised before she passed it on to one of her adult children.

While Abby finished packing, she heard Mary's van pull into the garage. Breathing a sigh of relief, she retrieved Mary's suitcase from the bedroom, then emerged to find her sister and Finnegan in the kitchen.

The service dog wagged his tail, sensing the excitement of their impending trip. Though he was older than most service dogs, Finnegan was always ready for action.

"I didn't mean to keep you waiting," Mary said, rolling her wheelchair toward Abby. "The shop is doing all the bouquets and arrangements for a wedding this Saturday and we got the wrong shipment of flowers. The bride was a little upset."

"I can imagine. Did you and Candace get it all straightened out?"

"It took a few phone calls, but the right flowers should be arriving tomorrow. If not, we came up with a backup plan that the bride approved."

Abby was glad to hear that. She didn't want anything to put a damper on their trip. "We'd better scoot or we won't make it to the dock in time to catch the ferry."

Mary moved toward the garage. "I'm ready. Blossom has plenty of food and water. Henry promised he'd look in on her for us too."

Blossom, the white Persian cat who thought she ruled the roost, never seemed to mind being left behind. She padded leisurely into the kitchen and sat down by her ceramic food dish, waiting for their departure.

Abby picked up both their suitcases, then they headed out to the garage where Mary's van was parked. It was specially equipped to allow her sister to drive despite her disability.

Abby loaded the suitcases into the van as Finnegan jumped inside and assumed his usual spot in the doggy bed at the back of the van. She secured him in the safety harness while Mary operated the mechanical lift that positioned her wheelchair in the driver's seat.

Once inside, Mary clamped down the brackets to keep the wheelchair in place, then waited for Abby to retrieve her bird painting from the house. Mary frowned when she saw her place the painting in the van.

"What's wrong?" Abby asked her.

"We're traveling by both land and sea to get to this antique show. I think you'd better wrap that painting more carefully or it might get damaged along the way."

"You don't think the brown paper is enough?"

Mary shook her head. "If it's a genuine Audubon, you don't want to take the chance that it might get bumped or dented, do you?"

"Of course not," Abby said, although she knew they didn't have a lot of time to fuss over wrapping it. "What do you suggest I do?"

"Why don't you grab one of those old blankets in the storage cupboard. At least that will give it some good padding."

Abby climbed out of the van and walked over to the upright metal cupboard that stood in one corner of the garage. It had belonged to Mary's husband, Jacob Reynolds, and held the tools he'd needed for his woodworking and delicate scrimshaw work. A professional writer, Jacob had loved working with his hands for relaxation and had taken up his carving hobbies with enthusiasm.

Along with Jacob's old tools, the cabinet held a couple of old quilts that Abby and Mary often took along with them on picnics. Frayed at the edges, the quilts had faded with time and had several small rips and stains on the fabric.

Abby grabbed one of the quilts and hurried back to the van. "Let's go. I'll wrap the painting while you drive."

Mary waited until Abby was buckled into her seat, then she backed out of the garage. The sun shone in the blue sky above them and Abby's heart picked up pace as they drove away from the house.

"I can't believe we're finally on our way. It seems like I've been planning for this trip forever."

"Me too," Mary said with a smile. "I can't remember when I've looked forward to a vacation so much."

"Oh, I almost forgot to tell you," Abby said, "Mom gave me Grandma Lora's locket to be appraised on the *Antique Adventures* show."

Mary's forehead wrinkled in puzzlement. "That locket isn't worth anything. It's just gold-plated."

"Oh, I know that," Abby replied. "And so does Mom. She doesn't care about the value, she just wants to get some insight into Grandma Lora's life."

Mary was silent for a long moment. "Maybe Grandma Lora wanted that part of her life kept secret for a reason."

"You mean you're not curious about her early years before she was adopted?"

"Of course I am. It's just that . . ."

"What?"

Mary shrugged. "I like to remember Grandma Lora as she was before she died. Content and secure in her faith. If we start digging into her past, we might discover something we don't want to know. Something that will tarnish all those wonderful memories."

"Something about Grandma Lora?"

"Not about her, necessarily, but something painful about her life." Mary glanced over at her sister. "She never wanted to talk about it. There must have been a good reason. Do we have a right to start prying into her past now?"

Abby was surprised by her sister's reticence. "I don't think having her locket appraised will reveal any deep, dark secrets about Grandma Lora. And if it gives Mom some comfort, I don't think any harm will come of it."

Mary pulled up to a stop sign, looking both ways before crossing the intersection. The dock lay just ahead of them, the blue water sparkling like diamonds in the sunlight.

"I suppose you're right," Mary said at last. "I guess that locket just makes me realize how much I miss Grandma Lora. She died over twenty years ago, yet I can still hear her laugh as if it were yesterday."

Abby smiled, remembering that contagious laugh and her sparkling blue eyes. "That's what makes me want to learn more about her. She was such a remarkable woman. She faced more hardship as a young child than most people face in a lifetime."

Mary nodded. "Yet, it didn't break her. In fact, she was one of the strongest people I've ever known."

"Me too," Abby agreed, studying her sister as she drove. "I've seen that same strength in you, Mary. In the way you faced your paralysis after the accident and fortified your own faith."

"That means a lot to me," Mary said softly. "I don't think I could have done it without your help. You gave up your job at Cornell and moved back to Sparrow Island after thirty-five years away."

"It was the best decision I ever made," Abby assured her.

She meant it too. Coming home to Sparrow Island had been the right decision. She had loved her years in New York, but it had been time for a change. She loved her new job at the conservatory and was grateful for the opportunity she'd been given to reconnect with her family.

They drove in comfortable silence, each pondering the past and the different paths their lives had taken. In that moment, Abby murmured a silent prayer for a safe journey and God's blessing upon them all.

WHEN THE FERRY from Sparrow Island reached Friday Harbor, Abby saw the *Victoria Clipper* already sitting in the harbor. Sunlight glinted off the white paint on the upper deck. The lower half of the boat was painted dark blue with a splash of red at the stern in the shape of the Union Jack. Over a hundred feet long, the vessel could hold almost three hundred passengers.

Hugo arranged for a cart to transfer their suitcases to the *Victoria Clipper* while Abby held onto her painting to keep it safe.

She inhaled the crisp salt air and a thrill of excitement coursed through her. Since she'd grown up riding on her father's boat, Abby couldn't wait to feel the spray of the water on her face and the exhilaration of flying over the waves.

"Are we all set?" Hugo asked, his blue eyes shining with anticipation. He had traveled around the world, but even a jaunt to Seattle still held excitement for him.

"Not quite yet," Mary replied, opening the bag on her lap. "I need to give Finnegan this pill the vet prescribed for him before we board the *Victoria Clipper*. It's supposed to prevent seasickness. My poor dog never has developed any sea legs."

Mary removed a slice of cheese from her bag and wrapped it around the pill. Then she held it out to Finnegan. He eagerly took it out of her hand, swallowing it in one gulp.

Hugo laughed. "Well, that was easy."

"Abby taught me that trick," Mary told him as they all headed for the catamaran. "Comes from all that experience with wildlife."

"She's the best," Hugo agreed.

Abby blushed at the compliment and couldn't stop smiling as they boarded the boat that would take them to Seattle.

The rest of the Sparrow Island group gathered.

"Is everyone here?" Abby asked Hugo, mentally counting the group.

"Everyone but Joe," Hugo replied. "He ran to the store to get some batteries for his radio, but he should be along shortly."

Born in Brooklyn, Joe Blackstock and his wife Margaret had moved to Sparrow Island twelve years ago. A down-to-earth man who had owned a printing business before his retirement, Joe didn't strike Abby as the kind to have any interest in antiques. Yet, he'd been one of the first to sign up for the trip.

"We might as well settle in," Hugo said, leading the group toward the lower deck.

The trip from the San Juan Islands to Seattle would span the one hundred and fifty miles in about three and a half hours. The *Victoria Clipper* could reach speeds of up to twenty-five knots and the clear sky and calm water indicated smooth sailing ahead.

Most of the seating on the lower deck consisted of tables and booths, with some bench seating available. They chose a table that was accessible for Mary's wheelchair, then Hugo lifted their suitcases from the cart onto the roomy luggage compartment above their table.

Finnegan sat beside Mary's wheelchair, his eyelids beginning to droop.

"Looks like his medicine is already starting to kick in." Mary caressed the dog's silky head. "Good thing he's off duty for the next couple of hours."

"What should I do with this?" Abby wondered, holding the quilt-wrapped bird painting in her hands.

"Is there still room in the luggage compartment?" Mary asked.

"Not with all our suitcases up there," Hugo replied. "It would be a tight fit and might get banged around."

A steward in a uniform approached Abby. "I see you have a rather large item. Are you by chance headed to the *Antique Adventures* show?"

"Yes, we are," Abby replied. It was easy to see they weren't the only ones. Many of the passengers were chattering about the show. Some even wore T-shirts with the *Antique Adventures* emblem printed on them.

"We have a locked cabin available to store the antiques," the steward told them, "if you'd like to use it."

"That sounds like the perfect solution." Abby turned to her sister. "Would you like me to put your scrimshaw in there too?"

Mary thought about it for a moment, then shook her head. "I think it's pretty safe in my bag. You go ahead. We'll wait for you here."

As Abby followed the steward, she saw Joe boarding the boat. Relief flooded through her as the large engines began to rumble beneath her. He'd made it just in time.

"Here we are," the steward said when they reached the cabin. "I'll need you to fill out this identification tag so you can reclaim your item when we arrive in Seattle."

He handed Abby the tag and a pen, then turned around to assist another passenger.

Abby filled in the tag with her name, address and phone number. As she waited for the steward to return, she pulled some twine from her bag to secure the quilt more tightly around the frame.

"What a beautiful vintage quilt," said a masculine voice behind her. "It's from the late twenties or early thirties, isn't it?"

She turned to see a tall man with dark hair and gray eyes smiling at her.

"Honestly, I don't know how old the quilt is," Abby replied. "It was made by my great-aunt Rebecca and has been in my family forever."

"Your great-aunt Rebecca had marvelous taste." He reached out to finger the fabric. "This fabric is indicative of the late twenties. I'm not an expert on quilts, but this is very fine craftsmanship, even with the minor damage."

"Thank you," Abby said, realizing this was another gift that she'd taken for granted. They'd stored the family quilt in the garage, along with tools and garden supplies, for as long as she could remember.

"So what do you hope to get for it?" he asked, sliding his hands into his pockets.

She stared at him, confused. "Get for it? What do you mean?"

"For an appraisal," he clarified. "Do you have a value in mind?"

She smiled. "I never even considered it. I just brought the quilt along to provide some extra padding for this bird painting that I want to have evaluated and appraised."

"Ah," he replied, amusement shining in his gray eyes. "So you have a treasure beneath the treasure. Intriguing. May I take a look at it?"

Abby unwrapped the painting of the gray catbird and turned it around for him to see.

The man studied the picture for a long moment. "Very nice lines and shadowing. The colors are exquisite. It's quite reminiscent of an Audubon, isn't it?" He looked up at her. "Or is it an original?"

"That's what I hope to find out in Seattle." Abby covered the painting once more. "I bought it at a flea market for only a few dollars, so I'm not really expecting much."

"I happen to be an antiques dealer," he said with a smile. "And I'd like to make you an offer I hope you won't refuse."

"What kind of offer?"

"I'd like to buy your painting on speculation. I'll give you a hundred dollars for it."

Abby blanched. "A hundred dollars? I only paid ten dollars."

He smiled. "Then you'll have multiplied your investment ten times over."

She laughed at his audacity. Despite his forward manner, the man had a charm that appealed to her. "I don't even know your name."

"Marcus Wolfe," he said with a small bow, "at your service. And you are?"

"Abby Stanton."

He smiled. "The pleasure is all mine, Mrs. Stanton."

"I'm not a Mrs.," she informed him, "and please call me Abby."

His smile widened. "Even better."

The steward approached her to retrieve the painting and identification tag, giving Abby a reprieve from Marcus's attention.

It had been a long time since a man had flirted with her like that. A flush burned on her cheeks and she needed a moment to compose herself.

The steward placed the tag on the back of her painting, then set it carefully in the cabin among the other heirlooms. When Abby turned around again, Marcus was still there waiting for her.

"Catbird got your tongue?" he teased. "I don't need an answer right now. Just promise me you'll think about my offer."

"All right," she agreed. "I will."

"Good," he said as the ship began pulling away from the dock, the engines humming. "It looks as if our journey is about to begin. I can't wait to find out where it leads."

CHAPTER ❦ FOUR

SEVEN SPARROW ISLAND residents gathered around a table on the lower deck as the *Victoria Clipper* sailed toward Seattle. Thelma Rogers, Joe Blackstock, Lindsey Buckminster and Naomi Yardley joined Abby, Mary, and Hugo at their table. Each had brought vintage treasures with them to have appraised at the *Antique Adventures* show.

They were a jovial group, laughing and talking as the boat picked up speed. Abby exchanged glances with Mary, both of them thrilled to finally be on their way. She had no doubt the next three hours would fly by with such good company surrounding her.

Thelma Rogers clapped her hands together to get their attention. "William Jansen wants me to write a feature story for *The Birdcall* about our trip to *Antique Adventures*."

William was the editor of the weekly island newspaper and preferred hard-hitting stories to fluff pieces. Abby was rather surprised he'd commissioned Thelma for this story, given her propensity to jump to conclusions about people.

In her early seventies, Thelma's thin gray hair was dyed blonde and permed into little cotton puffs on her scalp. While her take-charge attitude did make some people run the other way, deep down she had a good heart.

"So what I want to do," Thelma continued, digging into her large black purse, "is to conduct an initial interview with all of you about your hopes and expectations for the upcoming week."

"I hope my faience beads are worth five thousand dollars," Hugo quipped, "but my expectation is that I'll be lucky to get an appraisal of five dollars."

Everyone laughed, then began talking at once. Thelma pulled a notebook and pencil from her purse, then clapped her hands together once more to restore order.

"People," Thelma cried, "we must be organized about this or it will turn into pandemonium. Now, let's go around the table one at a time so you can tell me the item you're taking to be appraised, a bit of the background story and what you hope will happen at the show."

The group got comfortable, sensing this might take a while. Mary leaned toward her sister. "Thelma seems to be taking her job as a cub reporter very seriously."

Abby smiled. "Her feature story might take up an entire issue of *The Birdcall* by the time this week is through."

"Why don't you go first, Thelma," Hugo suggested, "so we understand what kind of information you want."

"Very well," Thelma agreed. "I've got half of an old tea set from Great Britain. My sister Betty is bringing the other half with her from Florida and we're meeting up at the hotel. It will be the first time we've been together in over ten years."

"What a wonderful reunion for both of you," Mary said, leaning back in her wheelchair.

Thelma nodded. "I can hardly wait."

Abby understood the special bond of sisterhood. She thanked God daily for bringing her back to Mary and her parents on Sparrow Island. The two sisters had never been closer.

Thelma flipped open her notebook. "I'd like you to go next, Naomi."

The softhearted librarian looked around the table. "I'm taking an old frontier territory map that I found tucked into a box of donated books. If it's worth something it would be a wonderful bonanza for the library."

"Map, bonanza, wild west," Thelma recited aloud as she scribbled into the notebook. "Next!"

Lindsey cleared her throat. She owned Summit Stables and loved horses. Abby had gone to high school with Lindsey on Sparrow Island and had always appreciated the woman's strong work ethic and integrity.

"I brought an old Meerschaum pipe that belonged to my uncle," Lindsey began. "He was a bachelor cowboy all of his life and left his worldly possessions to me, most of which had mildewed in the cellar where he'd stored them. The pipe is still in good shape though, and I thought it might be worth something."

"Pipe, uncle, wants big bucks," Thelma said as she wrote down the words.

"That makes me sound so greedy," Lindsey protested. "I just want to know its value before I decide what to do with it."

"Okay, got it," Thelma replied, adding more to her notes before flipping to the next page. "That brings us to Mary."

The light gleamed on Mary's silver hair as she moved her

wheelchair closer to the table. "I'm bringing a piece of old scrimshaw that belonged to my late husband. *Antique Adventures* is one of my favorite shows, so I'm very excited to be a part of it."

"I've heard of scrimshaw before," Thelma said, "but what is it exactly?"

"It's somewhat of a lost art," Mary replied, "begun by whalers in the early nineteenth century. They'd make elaborate, decorative carvings on whale bones and teeth and even walrus tusks."

Naomi gave a shudder. "I'm not sure I'd want a whale tooth or bone sitting around my house as a decoration."

Mary smiled. "It's very unusual and quite rare to find scrimshaw pieces anymore. Most of them are in museums, so I'm anxious to learn more about the piece that Jacob left me."

"So is it a bone, a tooth or a tusk?" Thelma inquired.

"It's a tooth," Mary told her.

Thelma bent over her notepad and muttered. "Whale tooth knick-knack."

Abby and Hugo exchanged smiles at the description.

Thelma licked the tip of her pencil. "Your turn, Hugo. You mentioned something about beads?"

"Egyptian faience beads," Hugo elaborated. "They were the early forerunners of glass beads and made of a mixture of powdered clays, lime, soda and silica sands. The Egyptians mixed this with a little water, then molded it around a stick to form a hard bluish bead with a hole in the middle."

"That sounds fascinating," Lindsey exclaimed. "Are they rare?"

He smiled as he shook his head. "No. In fact, they're still made in much the same way today. That's why I'm eager to find out if my beads were made a millennium ago or if the trades-men who sold them to me in Cairo exaggerated just a bit."

Hugo's deep voice reverberated with humor and warmth. He was one of the most interesting men Abby had ever met, and his vast knowledge and experiences made him the perfect curator for the Sparrow Island Nature Conservatory.

"Faience beads," Thelma murmured as she jotted the words down in her notebook, "Fancy fakes or the real thing."

Hugo chuckled. "Just in case they are fancy fakes, I brought along a signed volume by Robert Browning for appraisal too. He's one of my favorite poets."

"I didn't know we could bring more than one item." Thelma looked up from her notepad. "Otherwise I would have thrown in my collection of salt and pepper shakers."

"You can bring up to three items," Naomi confirmed. "My cousin went to the show when it was in Boston last May. This is the way it works: first they'll divide us into separate groups. So I'll be in the documents category while Hugo and his beads will be in the jewelry category."

"I'm glad I didn't bring that old Chinese wig stand," Hugo said with a smile. "I doubt there's a category for that."

"There is," Naomi countered. "It's called miscellaneous."

The group laughed, then Naomi continued describing the process. "They'll have an expert appraiser for each category who will give you a preliminary evaluation of your item and tell you if you made it onto the show. My cousin said the lines are endless, but it's a great chance to meet new people and just have a wonderful time."

"I can't wait," Mary exclaimed.

Hugo looked over at Thelma. "Don't worry about only having one item. Your tea set sounds like a marvelous piece of history."

"It is," Thelma agreed. "My mother had it appraised once for insurance purposes, but I'm anxious to see what a real expert has to say about it."

Abby had that same curiosity about her catbird painting and especially her grandmother's locket. She hoped the appraiser could provide one of the missing pieces to her grandmother's mysterious childhood.

"And what about you, Abby?" Thelma asked. "Do you have some kind of antique stuffed bird?"

"Well, it is a bird," Abby replied. "A painting of a gray catbird, actually. I found it at a flea market for ten dollars and I just couldn't resist it."

"One time on the show," Lindsey interjected, "I saw an old table that sold for two dollars at a garage sale and ended up being worth over twenty thousand!"

"Abby's ten-dollar painting might be an early Audubon," Hugo informed the group. "We're not sure, but it's very much in his style of painting."

"Catbird, flea market, ten dollars," Thelma said, using her unique style of shorthand.

Abby opened her mouth to mention the locket, but Thelma had already turned her attention to the last member of their group.

"Joe!" Thelma shouted to get his attention.

The seventy-four-year-old was listening to the radio. It was stuck in his shirt pocket with a wire earphone extending to his ear.

Joe looked up, then gave them all a sheepish grin. "Sorry," he said, pulling out the earphone. "The Yankees are playing in Seattle today and I wanted to catch the game."

Thelma arched a thin brow in his direction. "Surely you came on this trip to do more than listen to a baseball game?"

Joe chuckled. "I just needed a vacation more than anything else. So when Margaret suggested I take my autographed baseball from the 1947 World Series to the show, I jumped at the chance."

Abby was fascinated by the variety of their treasures and couldn't wait to see how they fared at the preliminary evaluation. She hoped at least one of them made it through the appraisal gauntlet and appeared on the show.

"Baseball, Margaret, vacation," Thelma recited, then closed her notebook with a triumphant smile. "Mission accomplished."

Mary glanced at Finnegan, who lay at her feet. "Looks like that medication I gave him really kicked in. The vet told me it might put him to sleep."

"Better asleep then sick," Abby observed as the group began to slowly disperse.

"Hold on a minute," Thelma called out. "We need to take a group picture for the newspaper. Does anybody have a camera handy?"

"I do," Abby volunteered, digging her digital camera out of her bag.

Thelma herded them out onto the open deck, then snagged a passenger standing nearby. "Would you mind taking a picture for us?"

"Not at all."

The familiar voice made Abby look up to see Marcus Wolfe holding her camera. His sudden appearance caused an odd flutter in her stomach, and she wondered if he'd been waiting for her.

"Okay, everyone." Marcus aimed the camera at the group. "Smile!"

Abby posed with Mary on one side of her and Hugo on the

other. The wind whipped her hair around her face as the boat sailed over the water and she could feel the excitement of the trip building inside of her.

"Perfect," Marcus exclaimed when he checked the picture display on the back of the camera. Then he walked over and handed it back to Abby as the group broke apart. "That's a very nice camera."

She placed it back in her bag. "I hope you're not going to make an offer for it too."

He chuckled. "It's not old enough for me yet. Now if you had a vintage Brownie, I'd be very interested."

They fell into step together, strolling toward the stern of the boat to watch the churning wake it left behind.

"But speaking of my offer," Marcus said, "have you thought about it?"

"I wasn't sure you were serious."

He stopped and turned to her. "I'm always serious where a pretty lady is concerned."

The man was a shameless flirt, but Abby couldn't help but like him. "I adore my catbird painting too much to part with it now, no matter what the value."

He nodded. "And I admire you for it."

Abby placed her hands on the rail, feeling more invigorated than she had in a long time. She didn't know whether to give credit to the fresh sea air or the handsome man standing beside her.

"Where are you from?" Abby asked him.

"Chicago, originally. I moved to Orcas Island five years ago and opened my antique shop there. It's always been a dream of mine."

"What did you do before that?"

"I was in the import/export business—a short leap to my new profession. I already had several contacts in the antiques world so it seemed like a natural fit."

"Did your job entail a lot of traveling?"

He nodded. "All around the world. Europe, mostly."

"And your favorite city there?"

"Rome," he said without hesitation. "Although I hate to admit that I usually spent most of my time in hotels rather than touring the sites. It's funny how you take things for granted when they become so familiar."

Abby nodded, knowing all too well what he meant. She knew a week away from her home and her work would make her appreciate them all the more when she returned.

"What about you?" Marcus asked. "Are you a native of the San Juan Islands or a transplant?"

"A native," she replied, "although I did live in New York for thirty-five years while I taught ornithology at Cornell."

"An ornithologist," he said with an approving nod. "So that explains why you like your bird painting so much. You must know all about the gray catbird."

"It is a fascinating little creature," she said, warming to the subject. Abby never tired of talking about birds. "Gray catbirds are mimics, which means they can vocalize a variety of sounds. Their most distinctive call is a catlike meow that gives them their name."

"Are there a lot of gray catbirds in the San Juan Islands?"

She shook her head. "Most of them winter along the Gulf and Atlantic coasts, then go as far west as British Columbia in the spring and summer."

"My, you do know a lot about them. I'm quite impressed."

"It's my job," Abby replied, "and my passion. I could talk

about birds for the entire trip if given the chance, so you've been warned."

He laughed. "You make it sound like a threat. I think it would be fascinating."

She blushed, amazed at how quickly the two of them had made a connection. She hadn't even known Marcus when she'd awakened this morning and now they were conversing as comfortably as old friends."

"It's easy to see that you feel the same way about birds that I feel about antiques," Marcus continued. He breathed a contented sigh as he gazed out on the water. "It's so wonderful, isn't it, to have a career that you love?"

"It certainly is." She inhaled the briny air and basked in the bright autumn sun as they stood together at the rail. The warm wind blew her hair around, but she didn't care. The boat ride was exhilarating and Abby was enjoying every moment of it.

"Look!" Marcus pointed to a whale breaching the surface of the water.

A pod of orcas stayed in view of the catamaran for the next hour. More people joined Abby and Marcus on the open deck to observe the magnificent creatures.

Watching them made Abby glad that whales were no longer hunted in America, though it had made the art of scrimshaw rare. Mary had told her that scrimshaw craftsmen now practiced their art on nut palm, which resembled ivory when polished.

As the orcas faded from view, Abby turned to Marcus. "Tell me what you love about antiques."

"The history," he said. "Each piece has a story. Some stories are fascinating, some mundane, but each one unique. Every time I acquire something new for my store, I start to gather as many clues about it as I can."

"So you're a historical detective?"

He thought about it for a moment, then nodded. "I guess you could say that, though I've never considered it quite like that before."

Abby understood. She enjoyed a little detective work herself on occasion. "Is that why you're going to the *Antique Adventures* show?"

He nodded. "I enjoy those venues the most. There are so many people and so many stories. It's like a banquet for an antiques connoisseur like myself. I simply can't resist the temptation."

She laughed. "Now I understand why you made an offer for my gray catbird painting. Are you more interested in the history behind it than the possible value?"

He chuckled. "I wouldn't go that far. I'm still a businessman. I just like to take a gamble every now and then. Even if it doesn't pay off, I enjoy the discovery process."

Abby thought about Grandma Lora's locket in her purse. Shrouded in mystery, the locket could hold the key to her grandmother's past. More likely, her search for more information would lead to a dead end.

"We're getting closer," Marcus said, as the catamaran made a sharp turn. "I can see the Seattle skyline on the horizon."

Abby took a deep breath, wondering what lay ahead of her. This was her favorite part of a vacation, when she was standing on the brink of a new adventure.

CHAPTER ❧ FIVE

THE BRISTOL HOTEL reminded Abby of a palace. Set in downtown Seattle, the twenty-story hotel featured several restaurants, a gift shop, two swimming pools, an exercise room and a fully appointed salon complete with hair stylists, manicurists and masseuses.

The vast foyer sported large marble columns and gleaming tile of terrazzo and granite set in a black-and-white diamond pattern. The nails on Finnegan's paws clicked on the floor as they headed toward the front desk.

They moved a little more slowly than usual since the dog still hadn't fully revived from the medication Mary had given him earlier. She kept casting worried looks in his direction, anxious to get him to the hotel room so he could rest.

Crowds of people bustled about the hotel. Many of them carried their treasured antiques in their arms or hauled them around on a dolly. Abby saw sculptures and furniture and all types of dishes and fragile glassware. One woman even hauled a life-sized doll.

"It looks as if half of Seattle showed up to have their treasures appraised," Abby observed as they finally reached the front desk. "It's a wonder they can fit us all in here."

After they registered for their hotel room and received their plastic key cards, the young woman behind the polished granite counter directed them to the grand ballroom.

"Can we settle into our room first?" Mary asked her, glancing at Finnegan.

"It would be risky." The clerk stood ramrod straight in her navy blue suit, her hair pulled back tightly into a neat bun. "If you're here for the *Antique Adventures* show you might not have enough time. They're conducting their preliminary evaluations right now. Once they reach a certain quota, they stop taking new submissions."

"We'd better not chance it," Abby told her sister. "We don't want to miss out on the show after coming all this way."

"You're right," Mary agreed, turning her wheelchair toward the open French doors of the ballroom. A long line snaked out of it, winding its way around the spacious hotel lobby.

They left their suitcases with the bellhop, then took their place at the end of the line.

"I wonder how long this will take," Abby mused, standing on her tip-toes to try and ascertain how many people were ahead of them.

The man in front of her turned around. He held a large, painted turtle shell in his arms. "This line hasn't moved in twenty minutes, so you two might as well get comfortable."

"At this rate, we'll be here all night," Mary said with a sigh. Then she gave her dog an order. "Sit, Finnegan."

He sat, plopping himself down on the tile with much less

grace than usual. His amber eyes looked glazed and his eyelids still drooped.

Mary usually didn't complain, but Abby knew that worry about Finnegan made her fretful.

"How's he doing?" Abby asked.

"Not too well." Mary reached out to stroke the dog's head. "That medication didn't agree with him at all. I'm starting to think seasickness would have been better for him than this. He's really out of it."

Abby checked her watch, wondering how much longer they'd have to wait in line. Perhaps she could check Mary's scrimshaw in as well as her bird painting and the locket so her sister could take the dog to their room.

More people joined the line behind them, then Abby heard a shrill voice cry, "What is a *dog* doing in this hotel?"

Both she and Mary turned around to see a large woman standing next to a skinny teenage girl. The teenager looked like she wanted to sink into the floor.

"I understood that this was a pet-free hotel," the woman continued. "In fact, I made sure to ask before I made reservations."

Her hostility was palpable. Abby looked at her sister, wondering how she would handle the situation. Finnegan didn't even seem to be aware that he was the subject of conversation.

"My dog is more than a pet," Mary said evenly. "He's a service dog and is legally allowed to stay here at the hotel with me."

The woman's brown eyes widened in dismay. "You mean he'll be here all week?"

"Yes," Mary replied, glancing up at Abby. "But I assure you that he won't bother anyone. Finnegan is very well behaved."

The dog looked up when Mary said his name and the woman stepped back a pace.

"That is not the issue," the woman said, bristling. "I was misled. I was assured this was a pet-free establishment and I intend to hold the manager to that promise."

The woman stomped off before Mary could say another word.

When the woman was out of earshot, the teenager stepped forward, her cheeks burning. "I'm so sorry about that. Aunt Susan doesn't like dogs."

Abby thought that was an understatement. She'd never seen anyone have that kind of reaction to Finnegan. Usually Mary had to fend off people who wanted to pet him while he was working.

"I'm sorry she's so upset," Mary replied, obviously shaken by the encounter. "Does she have allergies or something?"

The girl shook her head. "No. She just really doesn't like them. Aunt Susan isn't what you'd call an animal person."

My exact opposite, thought Abby. There was a difference between feeling uncomfortable around animals and the open hostility she'd witnessed. She mentally reprimanded herself for just standing there instead of defending her sister, too shocked to even open her mouth.

"I'm Amanda, by the way," the girl said, introducing herself. "Amanda Pederson."

"Nice to meet you, Amanda." Mary reached out to shake her hand. "I'm Mary Reynolds and this is my sister Abby Stanton. We're from Sparrow Island."

"That sounds like a cool place," Amanda replied. "Where is it?"

"It's part of the San Juan Islands, which are about one hundred and fifty miles north of Seattle."

"I'm from Montana," Amanda said. "Aunt Susan is my dad's sister and she invited me to stay with her for the week since I'm a home school student and we're on a break right now."

"Are you having a good time here?" Abby asked, wondering if that was possible with an aunt who exhibited such behavior.

"The best," Amanda replied. "There are so many cool people here and our hotel room number is the same as my birthday." She grinned. "I'm a leap year baby."

Amanda knelt down beside the drowsy dog. "Can I pet him?"

Abby was touched by the girl's sweet demeanor, which was so different than her aunt's abrasive manner. She hoped Susan Pederson calmed down about Finnegan's presence at the hotel. Traveling was difficult enough for Mary without having to deal with disgruntled hotel guests.

Mary hesitated. "I usually don't allow anyone to pet him when he's on duty because it might distract him, but poor Finnegan's not feeling too well at the moment, so I don't think it will do any harm."

One of the biggest problems Mary faced when she went out in public was people wanting to pet Finnegan. Abby couldn't blame them, the dog was adorable. But he was also trained to do a job and couldn't perform well if constantly petted by the people around him.

Some of them didn't even ask Mary's permission, but did what the staff at the training center called "drive-bys," where they ran their hand along Finnegan's back as they walked by him. If this happened too often, some service dogs became difficult to control.

"What's wrong with him?" Amanda asked, gently stroking the downy soft fur on Finnegan's neck.

"I gave him a pill for seasickness on the trip here," Mary told her. "It's made him very sleepy."

Amanda rose to her feet. "What exactly is a service dog?"

Mary smiled at the question. "Finnegan is specially trained to help wheelchair users like me. Some service dogs are trained to help the sight-impaired or hearing-impaired. Having a service dog helps someone with a disability become more independent."

"Oh." The girl stared at Mary's wheelchair.

"I was in a car accident," Mary replied to the unspoken question. "So I can't walk anymore. But with Finnegan around to help me, I can do almost everything else."

"How old is he?" Amanda asked.

"He's eight years old," Mary shifted in her wheelchair to stretch the muscles in her back. "That's old enough to be retired, but Finnegan likes his job too much."

"Job?" Amanda echoed. "Does that mean he gets paid for it?"

Mary smiled. "If you count love and affection and all the doggie treats he wants as payment, then the answer is yes. But the services he performs for me are truly priceless."

"What exactly does he do?"

"Well, he can open a door for me, then close it again. He can even help me pull my wheelchair if I'm too tired or sick."

"Wow," Amanda exclaimed. "That's pretty cool!"

"It sure is," Abby agreed.

The line had been moving at a snail's pace, but Abby noticed that several groups of people were now dispersing and headed in different directions. She was about to ask someone what was going on when one of the production assistants approached them.

His attention was on the clipboard he held. "I need your name and your item, please."

The young man looked vaguely familiar to Abby, making her wonder if she'd seen him on the show. Tall and lanky, he had dark brown hair and a neatly trimmed beard. The green shirt he wore was the same color as his eyes.

"Mary Reynolds," her sister replied. "I have a piece of scrimshaw."

"Okay, scrimshaw," he murmured, scanning the list in front of him. "That would be under the naval and boating category, which is now being evaluated in the adjoining conference room."

He tore off a red ticket stub from one of the many rolls in the bag he carried and handed it to her.

"Please go to the Conifer Room immediately," he directed. "You're number ten, so the wait shouldn't be too much longer."

"Thank you," Mary said gratefully, gently urging Finnegan to his feet.

Abby detected the faint echo of a Boston accent in the young man's voice and the impression that she'd met him before grew even stronger.

"We've got an old wedding dress from the last century," Amanda volunteered. "Where does something like that go?"

"Clothing is in the Aspen Room," the assistant informed her, handing the teenager a bright orange ticket stub.

Then he turned to Abby, his gaze still on his clipboard. "Item?"

"A bird painting."

"Art is in the Ponderosa Room," he replied, handing her a green ticket stub. "Three doors down and to your right."

"Thank you, Jeffrey." The name came unbidden to her lips. As soon as she said it, Abby recognized him. "Jeffrey Kugler. How are you?"

He looked up for the first time, his eyes widening in recognition. "Dr. Stanton?"

"It's been a long time."

"It sure has!" He shook his head in astonishment. "I can't believe you're here. Seattle is a long way from Ithaca, New York."

"I left my job at Cornell and moved back home to Sparrow Island to be closer to my family."

Jeffery Kugler had been one of her favorite ornithology students from at least ten years back. He'd grown a beard since she'd last seen him and no longer wore glasses, but his winning smile was the same.

"So how long have you worked for *Antique Adventures*?" she asked him.

"A couple of years now," he replied, holding the clipboard against his narrow chest. "It's not exactly in the ornithological field, but I'm biding my time until a job comes up. I still want to work with birds."

"Why don't you give me your address and phone number," Abby suggested. "I still have some contacts in the field and I'd be happy to give you a good reference."

His green eyes widened in surprise. "Really? That would be awesome."

Abby watched while he scribbled his contact information onto a sheet of paper, then handed it to her.

"I gave you my cell phone number, since I don't have a land line phone. Traveling with the show doesn't allow me to be home much anyway."

Abby tucked the paper into her bag. "Now where did you say I should take my bird portrait?"

"The Ponderosa Room." Then he grinned. "I should have known your heirloom would have something to do with birds. May I see it?"

"Of course." She unveiled it for him. "Can you name it?"

"It's a gray catbird," he said without hesitation. "And it looks like a great painting. Dr. Houston will probably go nuts over it."

"Dr. Houston?" she echoed.

"He's our resident art appraiser. The man is pushing eighty, but still going strong. His assistant, Chloe Cooper, is a good friend of mine. She's got a master's degree in art history with the intention of running a museum someday, so I'm not the only one who got steered off course in my career."

"I don't think there's anything wrong with putting some variety in your life or your career. You never know where that journey will take you."

"That's what I keep telling Chloe. And Ned. He's a camera man who majored in film studies at Columbia. And we've got Hans, a philosophy grad, in charge of scheduling." He grinned. "I guess *Antique Adventures* is just a melting pot of college graduates with nowhere else to go."

"It sounds like the perfect job for someone your age," she countered. "You get to travel and meet new people and you've probably heard lots of interesting stories about all the different antiques."

"Oh, I've heard some doozies," he agreed. "Don't get me

wrong, Dr. Stanton. I like my job. I do miss ornithology, though."

"Well, let me see what I can do about that," she told him. Then she remembered the locket in her purse. "I have one more item to submit."

"What's that?" he asked, consulting his clipboard once more.

"It's a gold locket."

"Jewelry will be in the Tamarack Room tomorrow," he told her, "during the second round of preliminary evaluations. We just don't have enough room or manpower to handle all the categories in one day."

"You do look busy," she observed, as more people joined the line behind her.

He nodded. "Too busy for me to stand around talking any more, although it's been a nice break. It's good to see you again, Dr. Stanton."

"It's good to see you too, Jeffrey."

"Maybe we can get together sometime this week," he suggested. "I'd like to hear about the work you're doing on Sparrow Island."

"That would be wonderful," she replied. "I'm in Room 348, so just give me a call whenever you have some free time."

"Will do," he promised, jotting her room number down on his clipboard, then moving to the next person in line behind her.

Abby sensed from the crowd of people surrounding her that Jeffrey would have very little free time in the next few days. She'd understand if he didn't have time to meet with her, although she always liked catching up with her students. She hoped she'd have a chance to see him again before she left Seattle.

As she headed for the Ponderosa Room, Abby came across Thelma Rogers pacing nervously back and forth in the hotel lobby.

"Hey, there," she greeted Thelma. "Have you already had your mother's tea set evaluated?"

Thelma shook her head. "My sister hasn't arrived yet. She was supposed to be here early this morning."

Abby could hear both worry and consternation in Thelma's voice. "Maybe her flight from Florida was delayed."

"I suppose that's possible," Thelma replied. "Or maybe she just decided not to show up at all."

Abby was startled by her words. "Wouldn't your sister call you if she'd changed her mind about coming to Seattle?"

Thelma pursed her lips as if struggling with a decision. Then she stepped closer to Abby. "There's something you don't know about me and Betty. We aren't close anymore like you and Mary. Truth be told, we haven't spoken to each other since our mother passed away ten years ago."

Abby hated to hear it. She valued her own family so much that it was hard for her to understand how a rift that deep could develop. "What happened?"

Thelma sighed. "Mama didn't leave a will and we both wanted her tea set."

Abby's heart sank at the thought of two sisters putting material things over their family. She assumed their estrangement wasn't about greed, but rather the pain they felt over the loss of their mother. Anger was a much easier emotion to handle than grief.

"So you've been estranged ever since her death?" Abby said.

Thelma nodded. "Mama promised that tea set to each of us at different times, so we both thought we had a right to it.

Mama grew very forgetful as she got older and probably didn't even realize it."

"So you each took half of it?" Abby surmised.

Thelma scowled. "That wasn't my idea. Betty just took off with the teapot and left me the cups and saucers. And right after the funeral too. It made me so mad at the time. I couldn't believe she'd do something like that."

It was hard for Abby to believe that the sisters had been angry enough over the tea set not to speak to each other for over a decade. Still, it wasn't the first time that she'd heard of siblings declaring war after the death of a parent.

For some reason those family heirlooms took on greater importance than their family ties. Or the death of a parent reawakened the sibling rivalry that had hibernated since childhood.

Abby knew she'd never let something like that come between her and Mary. Yet, her sister wanted to have Jacob's heirloom scrimshaw appraised for that very reason. Once she knew its value, she'd determine whether to leave it to her son Zack or her daughter Nancy and then give the other child something of equal value.

The last thing Mary wanted was her children fighting over her property after she was gone.

"Have you tried calling your sister to find out what's keeping her?" Abby asked, sincerely hoping their relationship could still be salvaged.

Thelma looked at her. "Do you think I should?"

"Absolutely. There could be any number of reasons why Betty hasn't arrived yet." She thought of her own sister's car accident and how Mary hadn't been able to contact anyone while trapped in that ravine.

"Maybe you're right," Thelma conceded. "I guess it wouldn't hurt to call her."

Abby watched the older woman walk off. She just hoped the tea set that had driven them apart could bring them back together again.

As she headed for the Ponderosa Room, Abby said a prayer for the two estranged sisters.

CHAPTER ✿ SIX

TELL ME YOUR NAME, YOUNG lady, and a little something about yourself," Dr. Houston said as Abby approached his table.

He was a small, wizened man with thick glasses and a mop of white hair that hung almost to his narrow shoulders. His red suit jacket had a small mustard stain on the lapel and a small magnifying glass dangled from the silver chain around his neck.

"I'm Abby Stanton," she replied, "and I'm an ornithologist and the Associate Curator at the Sparrow Island Nature Conservatory."

He smiled at her painting. "And you've brought me a bird. That seems fitting."

"I bought it at a flea market," Abby told him. "The owner had heard rumors that it was an early Audubon, but he didn't believe them. I was hoping you could tell me something about it."

"Well, let's just have a look." He studied the back of the canvas, then the front, running his fingers over the gilt frame.

"This is quite interesting," he murmured as he studied the painting. "Chloe, take a look."

Abby looked up to see a thin young woman with big blue eyes and dark hair. She stepped closer to Dr. Houston and took a quick glance at the painting. "Nice."

"You think so?" Dr. Houston winked at Abby. "I'm training Chloe to follow in my footsteps. The show thinks I'm getting too old for this job. If they ever succeed in replacing me, I want to make sure they do it with someone who's halfway capable."

Abby glanced at his assistant, wondering how she felt about the backhanded compliment, but the woman showed no reaction. She was probably used to the eccentric appraiser's manner.

Dr. Houston leaned closer to the painting, then a small gasp escaped his mouth. Without saying a word, he picked up the magnifying glass around his neck and held it up to the painting, carefully studying the canvas.

"You're in," Dr. Houston said, wincing a little as he straightened up to his full height.

Abby blinked. "What?"

"You're in the show," Chloe clarified as she reached for the clipboard on the table next to her. "I'll need you to fill out this release form."

"Just like that?" Abby asked. She'd been expecting the appraiser to share a little more information about her painting during the initial evaluation.

"Just like that." He glanced over at his assistant. "You'll need to schedule her taping on Thursday. And make sure her time doesn't conflict with anyone else."

"I know how to do my job," Abby heard the woman mutter under her breath.

Dr. Houston turned back to Abby. "And please don't forget to bring your bird painting with you. It always amazes me how often that happens."

"Do you really think it might be an Audubon?" Abby asked him, not certain if she could wait until Thursday to find out.

"My dear madam," Dr. Houston said with a lofty smile, "I cannot divulge that information yet. We must save it for the show. How else can we film an authentic reaction if our guests know the outcome ahead of time?"

"Yes, of course," Abby said, wrapping up her painting once more. She couldn't deny the thrill of anticipation that shot through her. Not only would she appear on the show, but she might actually own an authentic Audubon painting.

"What was your name again?" Chloe asked.

"Dr. Abigail Stanton," she said, deciding to use her formal title.

Chloe looked up at her. "You're a doctor?"

She smiled. "A doctor of ornithology."

"Oh." The young woman turned her attention back to the clipboard. "Are you staying here at the hotel?"

"Yes, I am."

"What's your room number?"

Abby gave it to her, as well as her cell phone number in case they had to get in touch with her about any scheduling conflicts.

"Okay, all you have to do now is sign the release form and you'll be good to go."

Abby took the pen from her and gave the standard form a quick read through before adding her signature at the bottom.

"We'll expect you here at ten o'clock sharp on Thursday morning." Chloe took the release form and pen back from

Abby. "I should warn you that you may have to stand around and wait on Thursday while Ned does his thing." She shrugged apologetically.

"The camera man?" Abby inquired, remembering her conversation with Jeffrey.

"Yes." Chloe heaved a sigh of exasperation. "He's always got to have the perfect angle shot and it takes forever."

"You're the one with the master's degree in art," Abby said, studying the young woman in front of her.

Chloe looked up at her in surprise. "How did you know that?"

"Jeffrey Kugler is a former student of mine. He mentioned both you and Ned to me earlier."

"Jeffrey really likes to talk about birds." Chloe set her clipboard back on the table.

Abby laughed, and Chloe smiled sheepishly.

"Okay," Chloe said. "I guess that's it. If you need anything or have any questions about the taping just give me a shout."

Then she moved to the side, going over her notes.

Abby blinked, wondering if Chloe literally meant for her to shout out any questions she might have. Fortunately, Abby had Jeffery's cell phone number tucked away in her bag if she needed any assistance. For now, she intended to enjoy her stay at the Bristol and look forward to Thursday morning's taping.

Hugo came up from behind her. "Well, how did your evaluation go?"

"Better than I expected." Abby couldn't hide her smile. "I made it onto the show!"

Hugo clapped his hands in delight. "Wonderful! Which item made it, the bird painting or the locket?"

"The painting. The locket won't be evaluated until tomorrow."

Abby was exhausted and excited. She couldn't wait to tell Mary the news.

"If you don't have plans for dinner," Hugo began, "our group is meeting at The Landmark restaurant on the top floor of the hotel. I'm told the cuisine there is excellent."

"I'd be happy to join all of you," Abby told him, her stomach already growling. "And I'm sure Mary will be too. What time should we be there?"

He checked his watch. "We're meeting at seven, so that gives us about half an hour."

Abby was surprised at how much time had passed since they'd arrived at the hotel. "We'll see you then."

They walked through the lobby and took the same elevator, Abby getting off on the third floor while Hugo continued on to his room on the eighth floor.

The plush beige carpeting in the hallway silenced her footsteps as Abby made her way to the hotel room. She slipped the plastic keycard in the slot, then let herself inside. They'd reserved a handicap accessible room, which gave Mary plenty of room to maneuver her wheelchair and provided counters at a lower height.

Mary and Finnegan were already in the room. The dog lay on his side on the bathroom floor, his eyes only half open.

"How's he doing?" Abby asked her sister in a low voice so as not to startle him.

"A little better now, I think," Mary replied. "I finally got him to drink some water."

"That's good." Abby bent down beside the dog, stroking

her palm over his soft head. "He probably just needs to sleep it off."

Mary nodded, though her brow creased with concern. "I feel so guilty for giving him that pill."

"It's not your fault," Abby assured her. "You were trying to prevent him from becoming seasick on the catamaran. No one could have predicted that he'd have this kind of reaction to the medication."

"Let's leave him here to sleep," Mary said, giving him one last look before rolling her wheelchair out of the bathroom.

When Abby emerged, she reached over to turn off the bathroom light, but kept the door cracked open.

"I called Dr. Federer," Mary said softly, referring to Sparrow Island's veterinarian. "He told me the best thing to do is just let Finnegan rest as much as possible tonight and he should be fine by morning."

"Has Dr. Federer seen this kind of side effect with that medication before?"

"Rarely," Mary replied, "but he said it does happen. As strange as it sounds, that made me feel better. Dr. Federer assured me that those dogs all fully recovered from their adverse reactions."

"That's good to hear." Abby glanced in at Finnegan, who was now sleeping on the porcelain tile floor. "Do you think he's comfortable enough in there?"

"That's where he headed when I released him from duty," Mary said. "I think the tile is cooler for him. It is a little warm in this room."

Abby looked around until she saw a thermostat. "We can adjust the temperature."

"I suppose."

The despair she heard in her sister's voice worried Abby. "What's wrong?"

Mary sighed. "I'm starting to wish I'd never come here. First, I had to deal with that rude woman in the lobby and now Finnegan is suffering. This isn't at all what I expected when we were planning our vacation."

Abby's heart ached for her sister. Mary had been looking forward to this trip to Seattle for weeks. She hated to think it could all be ruined for her in one day.

"Just give it a little time," Abby advised her. "We're both tired and hungry. We've been up since early this morning preparing to spend a week away from home. It's no wonder we're both a little frazzled."

Mary met her gaze. "Maybe you're right."

"I think I know the perfect solution." Abby opened the closet door and set her bird painting on the shelf above the clothes rod. "Our group's meeting for dinner at a restaurant on the top floor of the hotel. Let's just go there and relax and forget about everything else for a while."

"I don't know," Mary mused. "I hate to take Finnegan out when he isn't feeling well."

"He could stay here," Abby suggested. "He's sleeping now anyway and we won't be gone that long. I can help you with anything you might need."

Mary considered the idea. "It does sound like fun and I have to admit I'm starving."

"Then let's do it," Abby insisted. "After dinner we can come back here and get a good night's sleep. By tomorrow all three of us will be well rested and ready to face a new day."

"All right, you've convinced me." Mary rolled her wheel-chair toward the closet. "I need time to change first."

"So do I," Abby said. "We're supposed to meet them in . . ." she checked her watch, "about twenty minutes."

When they were ready to go, Mary refilled Finnegan's water dish, then gave him another pat on the head as he emitted a small snore from his spot on the tile floor. "I don't think he'll even realize we're gone."

Abby took a moment in front of the mirror to run a comb through her hair. Then she and Mary left the hotel room, letting the door close quietly behind them so as not to wake the dog.

"I haven't even told you my news," Abby said as they headed for the elevator. "They chose my bird painting to appear on the show."

Mary brightened. "That's wonderful. They chose Jacob's scrimshaw piece too. Nancy and Zack are going to be so excited to see one of their father's special treasures on the show."

The elevator doors opened and they moved inside. Abby was surprised to find the car empty given the amount of people in the hotel. She pressed the button for the top floor, then leaned against the back wall as the doors closed.

"Have you heard if anyone else made it onto the show?" Abby asked her sister.

"Naomi is the only person I've talked to and she made it onto the limbo list."

"What's the limbo list?"

"Well, I guess it's a waiting list of sorts. It's used to fill in empty time slots once all the evaluations are complete."

"Sounds like our Sparrow Island group is doing well. The

evaluation for Grandma Lora's locket is set for tomorrow. I guess with so many people, they don't have time to do them all in one day."

"I wouldn't hold out too much hope for the locket," Mary warned her. "I doubt a poor orphan owned anything of value."

Abby knew she was probably right, but it didn't matter. It wasn't the monetary value that interested her. It was the possibility of finally opening that locked door to their grandmother's past.

THE LANDMARK RESTAURANT offered a panoramic view of downtown Seattle. The skyscrapers were dark silhouettes against the pastel pink and blue sunset, the fading rays of the sun making Puget Sound shimmer as the light hit the water.

The Sparrow Island group was already seated around a large table when Abby and Mary arrived. Hugo had thoughtfully left a space open at one end of the table to accommodate Mary's wheelchair.

Abby sat down beside her sister, her stomach rumbling as she inhaled the savory aromas emanating from the restaurant's busy kitchen.

"The maitre d' recommended the salmon," Hugo told them, closing his menu, "or the beef burgundy. I'm sure both are excellent."

Abby ordered the salmon and Mary the beef burgundy, each intending to share their meal with the other and savor both dishes. Mary's melancholy began to lift as she conversed with the others around the table. Abby just hoped that Finnegan fully recovered so they could all enjoy the rest of their vacation.

"Where's Thelma?" Abby asked, looking around the table.

"We haven't seen her yet," Naomi replied. "I called her hotel room, but there was no answer. She's the one who made the reservation here, so I know she was planning to dine with us."

Abby wondered if Thelma had reached her sister. She hoped they could forgive each other for their disagreements in the past.

"I know Thelma will want a report about the preliminary evaluations for her feature story," Naomi said. "Why don't we just take some notes for her now so she can enjoy dinner when she gets here?"

"That's an excellent idea." Hugo pulled a pen from his pocket. "I'll even volunteer to be the scribe."

"And I'll go first," Naomi offered. "My map made it onto the limbo list, but I know the chances are slim that I'll actually get on the show. However, I did learn some things about cartography that will be valuable to me as a librarian."

"It's nice to know you got that far," Joe observed. "I struck out with my autographed baseball. Seems they've featured similar baseballs on the show already." Then he brightened. "At least I know it's authentic, since I was there when it was signed. I always feel so sorry for the people who get in front of the cameras only to find out their treasure isn't worth two cents."

Abby wondered about her own treasures. She wouldn't be embarrassed if the bird painting was a fake, just a little disappointed. She still loved the painting and would proudly hang it on her wall.

If it was an Audubon, then Abby had a dilemma ahead of her. Although she had told Marcus Wolfe she wouldn't sell it, she did have to consider that selling it could generate money for the conservatory.

As the others described their experiences, Abby learned that

Hugo had made it onto the show with his Robert Browning book, but Lindsey's pipe hadn't even made it onto the limbo list. Despite the rejection, she seemed as cheerful as ever.

Their food arrived at the same time as Thelma. She blew into the restaurant with a wide smile on her face. "Sorry I'm late."

She placed an order with the waiter, then she plopped down in a chair next to Hugo. "I finally reached my sister Betty and you'll never guess what happened."

"What?" Lindsey inquired.

"The silly girl missed her plane." Thelma shook her head. "Betty always was a little scatterbrained. I think that comes from being the youngest in the family."

"Do you have any other brothers or sisters?" Lindsey asked her.

Thelma shook her head. "It's always been just the two of us. I guess as the oldest, I've always felt responsible for her. That's why I insisted that she fly stand-by on the next available flight. Betty should arrive in Seattle some time tomorrow."

That news gave Abby hope for their reconciliation. "That's wonderful, Thelma."

"The best part is that our tea set made it onto the show," Thelma said. "I took my half to the appraiser today for the preliminary evaluation and told him the other half was on the way. He took one look at it and said we were in."

The group applauded her news, then Hugo handed her the notes they'd taken before her arrival.

"This is amazing," Thelma breathed, scanning the report. "Over half of our group made it onto the show and it's possible that number could go up if Naomi makes it off the waiting list."

They spent the rest of the dinner talking about some of the unusual antiques they'd seen so far. By the end of the meal, Abby was pleased to see Mary laughing and enjoying herself.

She felt as if a weight had been lifted from her heart and thanked God for simple joys like dinner with good friends.

Mary, Abby and Hugo lingered over coffee after the rest of the group had retired for the evening. Hugo entertained them with stories of his travels around the world until the restaurant was almost empty.

"We'd better go before the maitre d' kicks us out," Hugo said, rising from his chair. "May I escort you ladies back to your room?"

"We don't want you to go out of your way," Abby told him as they left the restaurant.

"I always like to take an evening stroll after dinner," Hugo said, "and I can't think of better company than the two of you."

When they finally reached their hotel room, Mary slipped the key card into the slot. When the green light came on, she pushed the wide door open and rolled her wheelchair inside.

Abby turned to Hugo. "Thank you for the escort. I hope you enjoyed your stroll."

He smiled. "Very much. Will I see you and Mary at breakfast tomorrow?"

Before Abby could reply she heard her sister cry out.

Both she and Hugo rushed inside the room. Abby's chest constricted at the panic she saw in Mary's blue eyes. "What is it?"

"Finnegan's gone!"

CHAPTER ✿ SEVEN

"H E CAN'T BE GONE," ABBY exclaimed, heading for the bathroom to see for herself. It was empty. Only Finnegan's water bowl remained.

"Maybe he's hiding under one of the beds." Hugo suggested, walking farther into the room to check for himself.

"He wouldn't hide from me," Mary protested. "I don't understand how he could just disappear. It doesn't make sense."

It didn't make sense to Abby either. She wondered if Finnegan had somehow managed to open the hotel room door, one of the skills he'd been trained to do to help her sister.

Abby walked into the bathroom, looking for any sign that might help her figure out what had happened to Finnegan. The medication had made him disoriented. Maybe after he'd awakened, he'd opened the hotel room door to look for her sister. It didn't seem likely given his extensive training, but Finnegan wasn't acting like himself and she couldn't think of any other reasonable explanation.

She stifled a groan at the thought of Finnegan wandering the hallways. Each floor was divided into three separate wings, along with short, dead-end passages leading to vending machines and stairwells. It was like a maze. If Finnegan had gotten out, he could be anywhere.

Even worse, Mary had taken off his collar, cape and harness to make him more comfortable while he slept. That meant there was no way to identify him if he somehow made it out of the hotel and onto the street.

Abby shook that unwelcome thought from her head. It was unlikely he'd even leave the hotel room, much less the hotel itself, especially without Mary. Besides, he'd barely been able to keep his eyes open all day. He certainly didn't have the energy to roam the hotel.

"He's not here," Hugo said, after checking under both beds.

"Do you think he got out of the room?" Mary asked, her thoughts mirroring Abby's. "I can't imagine he would do such a thing . . ."

Hugo moved toward the door. "We should probably search the floor. If the medication made him as loopy as you said, he could have left the room and be asleep at the end of one of the hallways."

Abby wondered if it could be that simple. She didn't have a good feeling about this, but they didn't have the first clue as to where to look for him.

"I'm going to call the front desk," Mary said, moving toward the phone. "Maybe someone has reported seeing him or can explain why he's not here." Then her face paled. "You don't think that Susan Pederson has something to do with this, do you?"

Abby hadn't even considered that possibility, but it made sense. Perhaps the woman had made such a fuss with the hotel manager that he'd forgotten about the legal ramifications and had Finnegan removed from the hotel premises.

"I'll go talk to her," Abby offered, then left Hugo with Mary.

She headed to the floor below, remembering that the girl had mentioned her room was the same number as her leap year birthday. When she reached Room 229, she took a deep breath, then knocked on the door.

A moment later it opened and Amanda stood on the other side. "Hello."

"Hello, Amanda. I'm sorry to bother you so late," Abby said, aware that it was almost ten o'clock. "Is your aunt here?"

"She's in the shower," Amanda replied. "Can I help you with something?"

"Finnegan seems to be lost."

"Oh no!" Amanda stepped out into the hallway. "Do you want me to help you search for him?"

Abby appreciated the offer, but she didn't like the thought of Amanda wandering the hotel alone at night. "I was wondering if your Aunt Susan made any more complaints about Finnegan."

The girl shook her head. "She's still kind of mad about it, but the hotel manager told her that he had to follow the law and that service dogs are allowed to go anywhere."

"That's true," Abby affirmed. "And it's actually a very good law. It allows my sister the same freedom as anyone else."

"I think it's a good law too," Amanda replied. "Aunt Susan is still getting used to the idea."

"So you don't think she's made any more complaints about Finnegan?"

Amanda stared at her, then understanding dawned on her face. "Oh, you think Aunt Susan had something to do with Finnegan's disappearance?"

"We have to consider all the possibilities."

Amanda shook her head. "No, Aunt Susan hasn't called anyone or even left the room. We've stayed in all evening because she was starting to get one of her migraines and has to lay down whenever that happens."

Abby nodded, half disappointed that they were back to square one. Finnegan was still missing and she had no idea where to look next.

"Thank you, Amanda," Abby said. "I appreciate your help."

"You're welcome." She stepped closer to Abby, her voice lower now. "Good luck with finding Finnegan. If there's anything I can do to help, please let me know."

She appreciated the girl's generosity. "I will."

When Abby returned to her room, the dog was still missing.

"What did the front desk tell you?" she asked her sister.

"Not much of anything," Mary replied. "They're sending the manager up here to explain the situation, whatever that means."

"The situation?" Abby echoed. That didn't sound good. "So they know what happened to Finnegan?"

"They wouldn't say," Mary replied as Hugo paced back and forth across the floor. "It's all so maddening. He belongs here with me."

Abby sensed this problem wasn't going to be solved easily. If necessary, she was ready to obtain legal counsel to assert her sister's right to keep her service dog with her. Too many people ignored the plight of the disabled, not realizing how much courage and determination it took for them to function on a day-to-day basis—to go out into the world and face all the obstacles in their way.

"Did you talk to Susan Pederson?" Hugo asked Abby.

"No, but I did speak with Amanda. Her aunt hasn't made any more complaints about Finnegan since the Americans with Disabilities Act was explained to her. She now realizes Mary has the legal right to have a service dog with her at all times."

Mary closed her eyes. "All I wanted to do was spend a week's vacation in a nice hotel. Why does everything have to be so difficult?"

Abby wished she could say something to make her feel better. She knew her sister was tired and terribly worried. No words could comfort her until Finnegan was back safe and sound.

"Why don't you call Henry?" Hugo suggested. "Ask him to look up the laws involving service dogs and fax them to the hotel. We may need to show them to the manager if there's a problem."

"That's a good idea," Mary replied. She retrieved her cell phone from her purse, then moved to the bathroom to make her call in private.

"That was a *wonderful* idea," Abby told him. "Henry can always make her feel better. He has a special way about him."

Hugo nodded. "If nothing else, it will keep her occupied until the manager arrives. If he's responsible for Finnegan's disappearance, he'd better have a good explanation."

Abby sighed. "I'm afraid this trip is turning into a nightmare for my sister."

"I've traveled enough to know that once disaster strikes on a trip, it often seems to have a domino effect. I remember one time when I was in Egypt and I lost my luggage, contracted food poisoning and got left behind on an expedition at the Great Pyramid all in the space of three days."

"Oh, dear," Abby exclaimed. "I'm surprised you wanted to keep traveling after that."

He smiled. "It took me a while to summon the courage again, but I'm so glad I did. I've come to cherish the memories, both good and bad."

"I just hope we can gather some good memories of this trip before it's over," Abby said. "Mary is so upset right now, I'm not certain she'll want to stay for the rest of the week."

Hugo placed a reassuring hand on her shoulder. "Once we get Finnegan back, she'll be all right. It's been a long day and we're all worn out. If there's one thing I've learned from my years of traveling the world, it's that sleep is just as necessary as food and water to keep you going strong."

Abby knew he was right. It seemed like such a long time since she'd been home, yet it was only this morning.

Mary emerged from the bathroom looking much calmer now.

"Feeling better?" Abby asked her.

"Henry always makes me feel better," she replied. "He was ready to hop on a helicopter and fly to my rescue, but I told him I could handle it."

"Good for you," Hugo said, then noticed Mary give a slight shiver. "Are you cold?"

"Just a bit." She pointed to the thermostat on the wall. "I turned on the air conditioner earlier so Finnegan would be more comfortable, but it's downright chilly in this room now."

"I'll get you a sweater." Abby walked over to the closet. She opened it and pulled out her sister's pink sweater. That's when she saw the empty shelf above the clothes rack.

"Is something wrong?" Hugo asked her.

Abby slowly turned around, a sinking feeling in the pit of her stomach. "Someone stole my catbird."

CHAPTER ❀ EIGHT

THE MANAGER OF THE
Bristol Hotel showed up at their door almost immediately.

"Hello," he said, introducing himself. "My name is Mr. Eames."

He wore a tailored charcoal suit with a white shirt and black tie. In his midforties, the man's dark hair was neatly trimmed and he had kind brown eyes behind his wire-rimmed glasses.

"Please allow me to apologize for any distress you may be feeling," Eames said. "I can assure you that your dog is fine."

Mary breathed a sigh of relief. "So you know where he is?"

The manager hesitated a moment, then nodded. "I'm afraid we had to call animal control after he bit one of our staff."

Mary placed one hand on her chest. "That's not possible."

Hugo placed a reassuring hand on Mary's shoulder. "Why don't you have a seat, Mr. Eames, and explain to us exactly what happened. In fact, why don't we all sit down."

Abby complied, aware that they needed all the facts before they could begin to understand the situation. She took a chair next to her sister. Mary's blue eyes were larger than ever in her pale face.

"Mr. Eames, I must tell you," Abby began, "that the bird painting I brought to *Antique Adventures* is also missing from this room. I believe there is probably a connection."

The manager frowned. "Are you sure?"

"Positive," Abby affirmed. "It was in the closet and now it's gone."

Hugo folded his hands on top of the table. "Perhaps if you start from the beginning, Mr. Eames, we can piece all of this together."

The manager took a deep breath. "It started with a guest complaint about the barking."

"Barking?" Mary echoed. "But Finnegan doesn't bark. He chuffs a little, but he's always good as gold when we're out in public. He's been specially trained as a service dog."

Eames raised his brow. "I confess I don't have much experience with dogs, service or otherwise. All I know is that it's our policy to immediately address any guest complaint, so I sent up my assistant manager to investigate the problem."

As he spoke, Abby wondered who might have complained. She already knew it wasn't Susan Pederson, but that made the whole incident even more disturbing. Did someone else take offense to Finnegan's presence at the hotel?

Abby always tried to have a good opinion of people, but this latest incident had rattled her. Judging by her sister's appearance it had done the same to Mary. Her slender fingers gripped the armrest of her wheelchair and her body stiffened as she listened to Mr. Eames.

"My assistant manager let himself into your room with a passkey when no one answered the door," Eames continued.

"He found the dog in an almost frenzied state. When he tried to grab his collar, the dog lunged at him and bit his finger."

Mary closed her eyes. "Oh no. This is my fault. That medication must have made him do this. Finnegan would never normally act this way. I knew he wasn't feeling right. I never should have left him alone."

Abby reached out to squeeze her arm. "No one could have predicted something like this happening. It's not your fault."

"Of course not," Hugo agreed, then turned to the manager. "Was the bite serious?"

Eames shook his head. "Just a little nip, actually. Hotel policy deemed it necessary for him to seek medical treatment. It also left me no choice but to call animal control. Unfortunately, we were unable to locate Mrs. Reynolds and let her know what was happening."

Abby closed her eyes, wishing they would all wake up from this nightmare. Abby knew that sick or wounded animals often bit in reaction to fear or intimidation.

Eames leaned toward Mary. "I want to assure you, Mrs. Reynolds, that I am aware of the federal law that allows you to have a service dog with you at all times. As soon as animal control determines that it's safe to release him, Finnegan will be more than welcome back at our hotel."

Mary sighed. "Thank you."

"Is there anything we can do tonight?" Abby asked.

Hugo looked at his watch. "It's already past ten o'clock. I can place a call, but I doubt they'll be able to release Finnegan until morning. At least I can make sure he's all right."

"Would you?" Mary asked him, wheeling her chair toward Hugo. "I'd feel so much better if I knew he wasn't sick or suffering right now."

"Of course," Hugo said gently, moving toward the telephone.

As they made the call, the hotel manager questioned Abby about her missing painting. "Are you certain it was in the closet before you left for dinner?"

"Positive," Abby replied. "I noticed it when I retrieved my jacket from the closet right before we left. It was tied together in an old quilt and very hard to miss."

He pursed his lips together. "I will question my assistant manager more closely about what happened when he entered your room. He was too upset to say much after the incident happened."

"I understand," Abby said. "I hope he starts feeling better soon."

"I'm sure he will. It's been a very stressful day for all the staff with the *Antique Adventures* show here and the hotel at full capacity. I . . ."

His voice trailed off and Abby could see the indecision on his face. She sensed there was something more he wanted to tell her. "What is it, Mr. Eames?"

He glanced over at Mary, who was intently listening to Hugo's phone call. Then the manager leaned forward and lowered his voice. "I didn't say anything before because your sister seems quite upset already."

"Say anything about what?"

"When the assistant manager came up here to check on the barking complaint he found Finnegan locked inside the closet. I wasn't sure if your sister had left him there or . . ."

"Of course not," Abby interjected, horrified that he'd even think such a thing.

"Now that I've met her, I can see that she loves her dog very much and would never treat him that way," Eames assured her.

"It seems apparent now that whoever stole your painting is the one who locked Finnegan in the closet. That's probably why the dog reacted the way he did when the assistant manager opened the door and reached in to grab him."

"We left Finnegan sleeping in the bathroom," Abby murmured, picturing the scene in her mind. "The thief probably didn't even see him when he entered the room. Finnegan must have come upon him and started barking while the thief was taking the painting out of the closet. So he just shoved him inside."

Abby recoiled at the thought of Finnegan trapped in the small, dark closet, already disoriented from the medication. Alone and frightened, it was no wonder he'd snapped at a stranger reaching inside to rescue him. In his altered state, Finnegan might even have thought it was the intruder.

"Do you have any idea who might have stolen your painting?" Eames asked her.

Abby shook her head. She certainly hadn't noticed anyone suspicious while she was standing in line for the evaluation or when she'd carried it up to the hotel room. Besides, it had been wrapped in the quilt most of the time, so very few people had even had a chance to see it.

"You have every right to call the police," Eames said slowly, "but may I offer a possible alternative?"

She looked up at him, intrigued by his words. "You don't want me to call the police?"

He hesitated. "As the hotel manager, I hope you can understand my position. It was quite a coup for the Bristol to host the *Antique Adventures* show. If the police become involved . . ."

Abby could see he was feeling the pressure on all sides, torn

between his duty to keep his guests happy and satisfy his superiors by making certain everything ran smoothly. Reports of a
theft might cause an uproar among his guests and make the
producers of the show very unhappy.

She realized that even if she did file a police report, they
probably wouldn't make the theft of a ten-dollar painting one
of their highest priorities.

"You have a possible alternative?"

He breathed a sigh of relief. "We hired additional security
as part of the contract negotiations with *Antique Adventures*.
The head of that security is a former police detective who I
can assign to investigate your case full time. Believe me,
Dr. Stanton, I won't let him rest until your bird painting is
recovered."

His fervent vow impressed Abby. Perhaps that was the best
solution, given the situation. The hotel was full of possible suspects. It would certainly be valuable to have someone employed
by the Bristol investigating the case. Someone who would have
full access to the staff and every corner of the premises.

"Bill Briley knows all the proper procedures," Eames said,
trying to sell her on the idea. "I'm sure you'll be impressed with
his thoroughness and expertise."

"Is he here now?"

The manager shook his head. "No, but he'll be here tomorrow. He can dust your room for fingerprints and . . ."

"That would probably be useless," Abby interjected, having
already considered the idea. "With all the hotel guests that
have been in and out of this room, there will be hundreds,
maybe thousands of prints. There's no way we could narrow it
down to the thief."

"I suppose that's true." Eames rubbed his chin. "Still, I'm
sure Bill will have some innovative ideas to solve this crime."

Abby had a few ideas of her own, but she'd need Mr. Eames's help. "Maybe we don't need to call in the police. At least, not yet."

His brown eyes widened with relief. "Oh, thank you, Dr. Stanton. The producers of *Antique Adventures* made it very clear that they'll only tape the show at venues of the highest caliber. There's even something in the contract about ending the agreement in the event of . . ."

"Criminal activity?" Abby ventured.

He nodded. "I'm afraid they'd consider the theft of one of the antiques as grounds for negating the contract. After all, without the antiques, they couldn't have a show."

Abby was beginning to wonder if the theft of her painting was connected to the show in some way. After all, how many people even knew she had a possible Audubon? Yet, the intruder had entered her room, gone straight for the picture, then left without disturbing anything else. Not even Mary's fine jewelry had captured the thief's interest and it sat in plain sight on the dresser.

All of this told her this burglary had been planned in advance. Since no crime was perfect, Abby believed if she started putting together the pieces of this puzzle she'd be able to solve it. Especially with the help of a seasoned police detective.

"All right," she told him. "I'll agree to your suggestion."

The manager rose to his feet. "I'm so glad this is all settled. I'll have Bill contact you first thing in the morning."

"There's one more thing," Abby said as they walked to the door.

"Yes?"

"I'd like to work with your detective on solving this case."

His mouth gaped in surprise. "Do you have any police experience, Dr. Stanton?"

"Nothing formal," she replied. "But since it's my catbird painting that's missing, I'd like to be involved in the investigation."

As he pondered her request, Abby saw she needed to convince him of the idea.

"I promise to be as discreet as possible, Mr. Eames. Certainly more discreet than the police would be if they were investigating this case."

He nodded, paling at the mention of the police. "You're quite right, Dr. Stanton. I'll be happy to accommodate you in every way possible. Just let me know what you need."

"Thank you," she said, grateful that he was so willing to work with her. No one would be as determined as Abby to recover her bird painting. Valuable or not, that gray catbird held a special place in her heart.

Hugo hung up the telephone and turned around to make his report. "Finnegan's fine," he said. "He's sleeping and has calmed down considerably. Unfortunately, they won't release him without proof of a current rabies vaccination, so we'll have to contact his veterinarian."

"I'll call Dr. Federer first thing in the morning." Mary turned to the hotel manager. "Can we have him fax the records here?"

Eames nodded. "Of course. And we'll be happy to provide a courtesy van to take you to animal control to pick up Finnegan."

Abby walked over to her sister and put her arms around her for a hug. "I'm so sorry you have to deal with all of this."

Mary gave her a warm squeeze. "I'm feeling better, Abby, truly, now that I know Finnegan is fine."

"Once you have the vet records in hand, you'll be able to pick him up," Hugo assured her. "I already told the animal control officer to expect us bright and early."

Eames moved toward the door. "I'll have my staff send up a fruit basket for all your trouble. Please let me know if there's anything else I can do."

"Thank you," Mary said, some of the color returning to her cheeks.

Abby followed Eames into the hallway. "I'll look forward to hearing from Mr. Briley in the morning."

"Thank you, again, Dr. Stanton, for your cooperation in this matter."

She watched him disappear into the elevator, then stood alone in the hallway. Closing her eyes, Abby let the events of the day drift through her mind, waiting for the peace that passes all understanding.

"Heavenly Father," she prayed softly, "Comfort my sister as she deals with the obstacles of her disability. Guide me as I search for the truth and bless us both as we try to live our faith. Amen."

She opened her eyes, feeling a renewal of her spirit and the peace that she'd sought. Her faith had carried her through difficult times before and would do so again.

Hugo left a short time later, offering to escort Mary to the animal control center in the morning before he bid them both good night.

Abby watched her sister prepare for bed. "I never realized before how some people treat you differently because of your disability. I keep thinking about Amanda's aunt complaining about your bringing Finnegan into the hotel. She was so hostile."

"I don't run into those kinds of people too often," Mary admitted. "But it does happen. Mostly, they're afraid, I guess."

"Afraid of what? That your paralysis is somehow contagious?"

Mary shook her head. "I'm different because I'm in a wheel-chair. That makes some people uncomfortable and they don't react well." She leaned forward to remove her sweater. "I actually feel sorry for people like that, to be honest."

Abby admired her sister's attitude, not certain she could be so gracious in the same situation. Then she remembered some of her own discomfort in adjusting to Mary's condition. She recalled her fears that she might say or do the wrong thing.

Her family and her faith had always helped her through the rough times. Other people didn't always have those same strong foundations to guide them through life.

As they prepared for bed, Abby updated her sister on the plan to investigate the theft of the catbird painting with the help of the hotel detective.

"I think that's the right move," Mary said, when Abby told her of the decision not to bring the police into the case yet. "It sounds like that detective has police training, and you've got some investigative experience yourself."

"I just hope it's enough to recover the painting." Abby pulled back the covers and climbed into bed, slipping in between the soft sheets.

Mary pushed herself up to the vanity table to remove her makeup. "At least you still have Grandma Lora's locket. What time is the evaluation tomorrow?"

"One o'clock." Abby yawned, weariness starting to overtake her as she grew warm and cozy beneath the covers. "I hope the appraiser can tell us something about the locket."

Mary smoothed moisturizer over her forehead, strangely quiet. At last she said, "I know something."

Her words startled Abby from her relaxed state. "You do?"

Mary slowly spun her wheelchair around to face her sister. "It was something Grandma Lora told me after Zack was born.

You know how she rarely talked about her experiences on the orphan train? This was one of the few times I ever heard her say anything about it."

Abby stared at her, amazed that she'd never heard anything about this before. "What did she say?"

"That she wasn't an orphan when she was put on the train. Her mother was still alive."

The news startled Abby. "Then why . . ."

"Orphans weren't the only children on the train," Mary reminded her. "The authorities gathered up neglected children too. Children who were running wild and living on the streets. There were also destitute parents who believed their children would have a better life without them."

"So Grandma Lora's mother . . . gave her away?"

Mary nodded. "She suffered from tuberculosis and worried about her ability to care for her daughter. So she made arrangements with the Children's Aid Society to find a new family for her daughter. A family that would care for her and love her."

Abby leaned back against the pillows, stunned by this revelation. "And you knew all this time?"

Mary nodded. "Grandma Lora made me promise not tell anyone, afraid the family would start peppering her with questions. You know how she hated to talk about those days. I think holding Zack just made her let down her guard for a brief time." Her voice thickened. "She spoke of how hard it would be to let a child go."

"Do you know anything else?" Abby asked softly.

Mary rolled her wheelchair closer to Abby's bed. "That wisp of red hair in the locket belonged to her mother. She allowed Grandma Lora to snip one of her curls before she left so she'd always have something to remember her by."

"You mean Grandma Lora never saw her mother again?"

Mary shook her head. "There was no way for them to communicate. Presumably she died from her illness soon after Grandma Lora left on the orphan train."

It took Abby a few moments to absorb these new facts about her grandmother. Her heart ached for them both, the little girl sent away to an unknown future and the mother who had selflessly given her away, hoping she'd have a better life.

"And you never told Mother any of this?" Abby inquired softly. "About where the hair in the locket came from or that Grandma Lora's mother was still alive when she boarded that orphan train?"

"No." Mary sighed. "I kept my promise to Grandma Lora until this moment. She didn't want anyone to know, fearing they'd think badly of her mother. She loved her so much."

"You have to tell Mom now," Abby said, her heart aching for their mother. "I think she deserves to know."

"So do I," Mary agreed. "I guess I've been putting it off, afraid to cause Mom more pain. She has such a tender heart."

"I know," Abby whispered, aware that her sister's heart was just as tender.

Mary wiped away a lone tear. "After so many years had gone by, I was afraid no one in the family would understand why I hadn't said something sooner."

Abby reached for her hand. "Why did you decide to tell me now?"

"I don't know." Mary sounded a little perplexed herself. "Maybe it's been a secret long enough. I didn't realize until Mom gave you the locket just how eager she was for information about Grandma Lora's past. Now if the appraiser doesn't give us any additional information about the locket, we'll still have something to tell her."

And knowing Ellen Stanton, Abby thought to herself, she'd hold no resentment toward Mary for keeping Grandma Lora's secret for so long.

As they lay in bed that night, neither Abby nor Mary could sleep. The events of the day and the past intermingled in their minds, until finally Mary leaned up on her elbows in frustration.

"I'm so tired, yet I can't fall asleep."

"Neither can I," Abby said from her bed. "Any suggestions?"

Mary thought about it for a moment. "We could order hot milk from room service."

"I have a better idea," Abby fluffed up her pillow. "Why don't we say a prayer together? The prayer that Grandma Lora taught us, since she's on our minds tonight."

Mary nodded, then folded her hands in her lap and bowed her head. Abby followed suit.

"Dearest Lord Jesus," they intoned together. "Thank you for bringing us through the day, protecting us through the night and loving us for eternity. Amen."

Mary lay back against her pillow, pulling the covers up to her chin. Then she emitted a long yawn. "I think I can sleep now."

"Me too," Abby agreed, her eyelids drooping. She settled into the bed and drifted off with the image of her grandmother reciting that same prayer to herself as she left her beloved mother behind and rode the orphan train into the unknown.

CHAPTER ❧ NINE

THE NEXT MORNING, HUGO accompanied Mary to pick up Finnegan from the animal control facility while Abby started her investigation. She headed straight for the front desk, eager to discover who had called to complain about the barking.

"May I help you?" asked the young female clerk with a nametag that read Marnie.

"My name is Dr. Abigail Stanton and I'm staying in Room 348. There was a complaint about a dog barking in my room last night and I'd like to know who made it."

"I'm sorry," Marnie said with an apologetic smile. "We can't give out names or room numbers of our guests for security purposes."

Abby explained her conversation with Mr. Eames the night before and his promise to extend full cooperation with her investigation.

"Oh," Marnie said, taken aback. "Mr. Eames left already. Let me get the day manager for you."

A few moments later, a woman close to Abby's age arrived wearing a plum suit and a cool smile. "I understand you need some information. Hotel policy forbids me from giving you a name. However . . ."

The woman looked around her to make certain no one was listening before she continued. "I can tell you that the caller complained that a dog was barking in the next room, if that's helpful."

"It is," Abby said, relieved to get that much information. She understood the tightrope the management had to walk to keep their guests safe and appreciated the fact that they were so diligent.

At least the information about the call narrowed down her search to the guests on either side of her room. Abby returned to the third floor and approached the door on the right of her hotel room first. She knocked once, hoping the occupants weren't still asleep.

The door opened a crack, the chain lock still attached. An elderly woman peered out through the slant. "Yes? Who is it?"

"I'm Abby Stanton and I'm staying in the room next to you. I was hoping you could tell me if you heard a dog barking in my room last night."

The woman shook her head. "I didn't hear a sound. I always bring my earplugs to hotels and I sleep like a baby."

"Well, I'm glad the dog didn't disturb you," Abby said with a smile. "Thank you."

The woman closed the door, leaving Abby with only one other option. Taking a deep breath, she approached the door to the left of her hotel room and knocked. This had to be the one who had made the complaint, so she wasn't sure what to expect.

A moment later the door opened and a small man with skin the color of warm cocoa stood on the other side. "May I help you?"

"My name is Abby Stanton and I'm in the room right next to yours. I'd like to talk to you about the dog barking incident last night."

"Oh." He hesitated. "I'm the one who called the front desk about it. Does the dog belong to you?'

"My sister," Abby clarified. "He's a service dog."

"I see." He opened the door wider. "My name is Tate Okafor. Won't you come in?'

Abby walked inside the room, noticing that his packed suitcases stood close to the door. It looked as if Mr. Okafor was checking out today.

"I'm sorry to bother you," Abby began, "this shouldn't take long."

"Not to worry," Mr. Okafor replied. "My ride to the airport doesn't leave for a few minutes yet." He motioned toward the table and chairs. "Please, have a seat."

Abby pulled out a chair and sat down. She noticed that he'd left the door standing wide open so she wouldn't feel uncomfortable alone in the hotel room with him. She was mildly surprised at this considerate behavior given his complaint about Finnegan.

"Since you're leaving today," Abby began, "that must mean you're not here for the *Antique Adventures* show?"

He chuckled. "No, I was attending an electronics convention at the conference and trade center. I was actually quite surprised when I arrived at the Bristol and found all this commotion. If I'd known about it in advance I would have booked another hotel."

"It is pandemonium," Abby agreed. "Although I rather

enjoy all the hustle and bustle. I had no idea so much work went into the show."

"I'm sorry to admit I rarely watch it." He leaned back in his chair. "I travel so much that I don't have much time for television."

"I know you must be very busy," Abby told him. "The reason I'm here is that someone broke into my hotel room last night. I believe that's the reason my sister's dog started barking."

"That would explain it," Mr. Okafor said slowly. "At the time, I assumed some inconsiderate guest had snuck a dog into their room, since this is a pet-free hotel. Normally, the barking wouldn't have bothered me, but I leave for Japan today, so I wanted to get a good night's sleep to help ward off jet lag."

"I understand." Abby found herself liking the man, a reaction she hadn't expected. "Can you tell me exactly what happened last night?"

Mr. Okafor pondered the question for a moment. "I'd just finished washing up before bed when I heard the barking. I thought it was odd, but initially assumed it was coming from a television somewhere. Then the barking grew even louder, so I called the front desk to tell them about it."

"How did you know which room it was coming from?"

"Oh," he said, "I forgot to tell you that before I placed the call to the front desk I walked down the hall until I reached your door. The barking was definitely coming from inside."

"Did you hear anything else inside my room?"

He shook his head. "No, not a thing. Of course, the barking was quite loud."

Abby surmised that Finnegan had been shut in the closet at that point, so the intruder could escape. "Did you happen to see anyone in the hallway?"

"No," he began, then hesitated. "Wait a minute. I did see a

maid pushing one of those carts. She passed me as I walked toward your room."

"Can you describe her for me?"

He grimaced. "I really wasn't paying much attention, I'm afraid. I'd say she was average height and weight. She wore one of those gray uniforms like all the other maids, so nothing about her really stood out to me. I was more focused on locating the room with the dog."

Abby had hoped he could be more specific. The maid might be a witness to the crime and be able to identify the intruder. "Is there anything else about her that you remember? The color of her hair or eyes? Any identifying marks or scars?"

He thought for a long moment. "I know she had dark hair that hung to her shoulders. In fact, now that I think about it, I'd say that was a little unusual. I've noticed most of the maids wear their hair neatly pulled back, but this maid's hair hung around her face, almost covering half of it."

It wasn't much, but it was something. She rose to her feet. "Thank you, Mr. Okafor. I really appreciate your help."

"I wish I could do more," he said wistfully.

"Maybe you can," she said, taking him up on his offer. "As someone in the electronics field, do you know anything about hotel room locks?"

"A little," he replied. "I never imagined a place like the Bristol would be vulnerable to a thief. Did he jimmy the lock in some way?"

She shook her head. "The assistant manager saw nothing unusual about the door mechanism."

"Then the thief must have used a master key card," Mr. Okafor said. "The hotel should have either a consecutive number system for their key cards or individual serial numbers on each card. That means it shouldn't take them long to determine if one of them is missing."

Abby appreciated the information. "I'll definitely ask the hotel detective about it. If we can trace who the missing card belongs to, we might be able to determine who took it."

Mr. Okafor walked her to the door. "I'd like to apologize for any inconvenience my phone call might have caused last night. If I'd known all the circumstances of the situation I never would have made that telephone call."

She appreciated his apology and hastened to reassure him. "It's not your fault. We believe the combination of the intruder and a reaction to some medication Finnegan had taken made him act completely out of character. He was removed from the hotel by animal control for nipping the finger of one of the hotel staff, not for barking."

Mr. Okafor sighed. "That is a shame. Hopefully, the dog will be reunited with your sister soon."

"She's on her way to pick him up now."

The elevator doors opened across from them and a bellhop emerged pushing a luggage cart.

"Looks like it's time for me to go." Mr. Okafor directed the bellhop into his room.

"Thank you again for all your help," Abby told him. "Have a good trip to Japan."

He waved good-bye to her as Abby headed to her room. Now she just needed to track down the maid who had been in the hallway last night.

When she opened the door to her room, Finnegan bounded up to her, his tail wagging.

"Finnegan!" She exclaimed, bending down to give the dog a hug. "You're back!"

"We just got here," Mary said, rolling her wheelchair closer to them. "Doesn't he look good?"

"He looks great," Abby concurred. "Fully recovered from that nasty pill and his night at the animal control facility."

"You should have seen how excited he was when I picked him up. He's definitely got his energy back." Mary reached out to scratch him under the collar. "I promised him we'd never be apart that long again."

Abby said a silent prayer of thanks that Finnegan had been returned to them safe and sound. The faithful dog had tried to protect them when the intruder entered the room and he had suffered for it. Abby planned to get him a special treat before the week was over.

"So what's on your schedule for today?" Mary asked her.

"I plan to meet with the hotel detective soon. Hopefully, we can compare notes and go from there. I already met with the man who complained about Finnegan's barking last night. His name is Mr. Okafor and he's truly sorry for all the trouble it caused."

Mary nodded. "I'm not as upset about it as I was last night. The series of events with the medication and the intruder were things no one could have foreseen." She reached down to nuzzle Finnegan's face. "But I still don't intend to let you out of my sight today, pal."

"What are you plans?" Abby asked.

Mary gave her a tired smile. "Believe it or not, I think I need a nap. I barely slept last night and I'm worn out. So Finnegan and I are going to spend most of the day here in the room just relaxing."

Abby was glad to hear it. Her sister needed time to recover from the traumatic events of yesterday and regain her energy.

"Maybe we can order room service later and have lunch here together," Abby suggested.

Mary winced. "That's so terribly expensive, even though it is very tempting."

"I know it costs a little more than going to one of the restaurants," Abby said, usually more frugal with her money. "But let's splurge just this once to celebrate Finnegan's return. We can kick off our shoes and have a leisurely meal."

Mary heaved a contented sigh. "That sounds perfect to me."

Abby left her sister and Finnegan resting in the hotel room while she headed to the main lobby to meet with the detective. A clerk at the front desk directed her to his office. She was surprised to find the door locked and no sign of anyone inside.

She approached the clerk again. "I'm sorry to bother you, but I'm looking for Bill Briley."

"He's not in his office?" the young man asked.

"No." Abby leaned against the counter. "I was supposed to meet with him this morning."

"One moment, please," the young man said as he tapped the keyboard in front of him, then waited for a new screen to pop up. "According to Mr. Briley's online schedule, he's in the hotel somewhere. Would you like to leave a message for him?"

Abby wasn't sure what to do. Mr. Eames had made it clear to her last night that he'd inform Mr. Briley about the theft and set up a meeting for the two of them first thing this morning.

So either Mr. Briley didn't get the message or he'd ignored it. She decided to give him the benefit of the doubt. "Yes, I would like to leave a message. Please have him contact Dr. Abigail Stanton in Room 348 as soon as possible."

"I'll be happy to do so," the clerk said. "I'll send him an

e-mail and leave a note on his desk to make certain he receives your message. And I'm sorry for any inconvenience this has caused you."

"Thank you," Abby said, hoping it wouldn't take long for Mr. Briley to get back to her.

As she left the front desk Abby saw Thelma walking toward her. She wore a bright pink wind suit and white tennis shoes.

"Good morning," Thelma said, grasping Abby by the elbow and pulling her off to one side. "I just saw Hugo in the coffee shop and he mentioned the awful ordeal you and Mary went through last night. I can't believe your bird painting was stolen!"

"I'm afraid it's true."

Thelma clucked her tongue. "I told Betty that I don't know what this world's coming to when a thief can break into your hotel room while you're having dinner. It's as if no place is safe anymore."

"Is Betty here?" Abby asked, happy to hear the sisters were talking.

Thelma grinned. "She arrived early this morning. I haven't actually seen her yet because she wants a chance to freshen up, but we had a long talk on the telephone. It was just like old times."

Abby's heart warmed at the news. She couldn't remember the last time she'd seen Thelma look this happy.

"Will you do me a favor?" Thelma asked her, running her fingers through her blonde curls.

"If I can."

"I brought a special picture as a gift for Betty and I want to pick out just the right frame." Thelma pointed toward the gift shop. "I've narrowed it down to a couple of choices, but I could really use a second opinion if you have a few minutes."

"Of course I do," Abby said. "I'll be happy to help you."

She followed Thelma inside the gift shop. It was full of souvenirs as well as T-shirts, books, and toiletries one might need while traveling. The picture frames occupied almost the entire back wall of the store.

"This is quite a selection," Abby said, surveying the variety of frames in front of her. "I can see why you'd have trouble choosing just one."

Thelma fumbled inside the large black bag she always carried. "Let me show you the picture first."

Abby watched her retrieve a small cardboard envelope out of her bag. Then she carefully removed an old photograph from the envelope. "This is a picture of my mother with Betty and me when we were children. It's hard for me to believe it was taken over sixty years ago."

Abby leaned over the woman's shoulder for a closer look. She never would have recognized the pigtailed Thelma standing beside her mother. The little girl couldn't have been more than seven years old, judging by her freckles and gap-toothed smile. Her younger sister Betty stood beside her, barely reaching Thelma's shoulder.

"You can see Mama's tea set on the table in front of us," Thelma pointed out. "That was her most prized possession."

"Your mother was a very pretty woman," Abby observed.

"Yes, she was," Thelma said proudly. "She always kept herself up well. Mama believed that a lady should never look frazzled." Then she laughed. "I can't say I've followed that same fashion philosophy very well myself."

"It's a wonderful picture. I'm sure your sister will be thrilled with the gift."

A shadow of sadness darkened Thelma's green eyes. "I still

can't believe we let so much time pass without speaking to each other. Mama would have been so disappointed in us."

"At least now you're making amends," Abby said before turning back to the picture frames. "So which ones appeal to you?"

"I really like this pewter one." Thelma reached up to take the frame off the shelf. "But I also like the blue ceramic frame. Which do you think?"

Abby studied both frames, then held the old photograph by each one.

"I like the pewter one the best," Abby said at last. "The antique finish and the style of the frame seem to fit the era of the picture. Plus, it won't be quite as fragile for Betty's long trip home as the ceramic picture frame. That one could break or chip so easily."

"You've got a point." Thelma placed the blue frame back on the shelf. "The pewter one it is, then. I'm going to have them gift wrap it for me after I put the picture in it." She smiled. "I can't wait to see the look on Betty's face when she opens it."

Abby was happy to help. Selecting a picture frame was so much easier than sorting through suspects. She just wished she had a solid lead to push her in the right direction.

CHAPTER ✿ TEN

ABBY DECIDED TO ACT alone on the tip from Mr. Okafor instead of waiting for Mr. Briley to contact her. With only four days left at the hotel, she didn't have any time to waste in her investigation.

A quick call to the hotel manager got her a meeting with the maid supervisor. They were bending over backwards at the Bristol to accommodate her so she wouldn't call the police about the theft. Abby still hoped that was the right decision.

She found Mrs. Gable in her office in the basement of the hotel. Abby had taken the service elevator at the direction of the manager and wondered if the thief had done the same after stealing her catbird painting.

"Please have a seat, Dr. Stanton," Mrs. Gable said. She was in her mid-fifties, with fine silver strands threaded through her jet black hair. Her brown eyes were warm and friendly as she walked over to the small coffee station in the corner. "The manager told me to expect you. Would you like a cup of coffee?"

"Yes, please," Abby replied, realizing she hadn't even taken time for breakfast. "And thank you for seeing me on such short notice. I'll try not to take up too much of your time."

As Mrs. Gable poured them each a cup of coffee, Abby took a moment to look around her neatly appointed office. If this was an example of Mrs. Gable's skills as an organizer, Abby had no doubt that the cleaning services at the Bristol were very well run.

Mrs. Gable handed a cup of coffee to Abby before returning to her desk. "Now, Dr. Stanton, how may I help you today?"

She wondered how much the manager had revealed to her about the theft. Since she couldn't be sure, Abby decided to start at the beginning. "My sister and I checked into Room 348 yesterday afternoon with her service dog, Finnegan."

Mrs. Gable's dark eyes widened with interest. "I must tell you that the cleaning staff are always surprised when they find a dog in the room. Those service dogs are so well trained and well behaved that they cause very little additional work for us."

Abby was glad to hear it, although she hoped at least one of Mrs. Gable's maids had noticed Finnegan barking last night.

"Last evening we left Finnegan alone in the room," Abby continued, "while my sister and I dined in one of the restaurants. Unfortunately, an incident occurred while we were out and Finnegan was taken into custody by animal control."

"My goodness," Mrs. Gable exclaimed. "What kind of incident?"

Abby was somewhat surprised she hadn't heard about it yet. Then again, the size of the staff at a hotel as large as the Bristol had to be enormous, so it might take longer for such news to make it through the grapevine. "Finnegan was barking at an intruder in our hotel room who then shut him into a closet."

"Oh dear," Mrs. Gable said. "Now that you mention it, I do remember hearing that one of the assistant managers got bitten last night. It sounded as if it was little more than a tiny break in the skin and the young man only needed one of those small bandages to cover it up."

Abby was glad to hear it wasn't more serious. Mary had mentioned wanting to find the injured man today and apologize for any pain he had suffered.

"Did the intruder take anything?" Mrs. Gable asked her.

Abby nodded. "A bird painting that I'd brought with me for appraisal on the *Antique Adventures* show. It was wrapped in an old quilt, which was also taken."

Interest sparked in her eyes. "A quilt? I do a bit of quilting myself. Do you happen to know the pattern?"

"I believe it's called log cabin," Abby replied. "It was very old and worn. I had tied it around the painting to keep it from getting damaged. Unfortunately, it didn't prevent it from getting stolen."

"Oh my," Mrs. Gable said, compassion in her eyes. "That must have been terribly upsetting for both you and your sister."

"It was." Abby took a sip of her coffee, impressed with the rich brew. "I talked to another hotel guest this morning who told me that he passed a maid pushing a cleaning cart near my room about the same time as the theft. I was hoping to speak to her and discover if she saw anyone who looked suspicious."

"Of course." Mrs. Gable swiveled in her office chair to face the computer on her desk. "You said this happened last night?"

"Yes. Around nine o'clock."

The supervisor began working the keyboard in front of her. "This is my duty list from last night. There were about sixty maids working the evening shift."

Abby set her coffee cup on the table beside her. "How many on my floor?"

"You're in Room 348, is that correct?"

"Yes."

Mrs. Gable scrolled down the page on the computer screen in front of her. "I had two maids assigned to that floor, Juanita Perez and Bethany Hawser. "I can call them up here if you'd like to talk with them."

"Before you do," Abby said, "can you describe them for me?"

Mrs. Gable thought for a moment. "Juanita's an older woman with gray hair and a slight limp due to a bad hip. She's getting close to retirement. Bethany's quite a bit younger, but a very shy girl. She's quite heavy for her height and has curly blonde hair."

Abby swallowed a sigh of disappointment. "I'm afraid neither of those women fit the description of the maid my witness observed. Is it possible another maid was on that floor?"

"It would be highly unusual." Mrs. Gable looked at her list again. "Perhaps if you describe the maid the witness saw last night, I can help narrow down the possibilities."

Abby almost hated to give her the generic description, sensing it would be futile. "He said she was average height and weight and had shoulder-length dark hair."

Mrs. Gable swiveled in her chair to face Abby. "That description fits over half of my staff and I employ over one hundred and eighty maids."

"I was afraid of that." Abby picked up her coffee cup again and took another sip. The brew was tepid now, but still tasted good. "Oh, I almost forgot. The witness said this maid wore her hair down and it covered half of her face."

Mrs. Gable shook her head. "We have a strict uniform code

here and that includes wearing long hair pulled back from the face and secured with a clip or a ponytail holder. Any one of my cleaning staff caught with his or her hair hanging down like that would receive an official reprimand."

Abby was beginning to wonder if this maid even existed. She was tempted to ask Mrs. Gable for pictures of her staff, but Mr. Okafor was probably already on his plane to Japan and he was the only one who could identify her.

She had hit a dead end. Abby stood up, wondering what to do next. "Thank you for your time, Mrs. Gable, and for the delicious coffee."

"You're very welcome." The supervisor escorted her to the door. "I'm so sorry I couldn't be more help to you, Dr. Stanton. I'll definitely keep my eyes and ears open, though. If I hear anything about your painting, I'll let you know."

"I'd appreciate it."

She was halfway out the door when Mrs. Gable called her back.

"Dr. Stanton?"

"Yes?"

"Can you describe your bird painting for me? I'll print up a flyer for the maids. It's possible one of them may come across it or the quilt while they're cleaning."

Abby thought that was an excellent idea. "It's a painting of a gray catbird, which is a little bird with gray feathers. In the painting he's perched on a branch. The gold frame is twenty-four inches square and chipped at the corners."

"I'll type that flyer up immediately and give one to each of my cleaning staff before they make their rounds. If it's in one of these hotel rooms, there's a good chance they'll see it."

Abby hoped it could be that easy. However, that possibility

did trigger another question she hoped Mrs. Gable could answer. "How does your staff enter all the rooms they're assigned to clean? Do they carry a master key card of some sort?"

"Yes. Each master key is designed to open any door in the hotel. However, they are kept very safely guarded. Each one of my staff must check a master key card out when they come on duty, then check it back in before they finish their shift."

"So there are no stray master keys floating around that you know about?"

Mrs. Gable flashed a confident smile. "Not on my watch."

Abby believed her, but it still didn't explain how the intruder had entered her hotel room. "Thank you again, Mrs. Gable."

"You're welcome. Please let me know if I can be of any further assistance."

As Abby rode the elevator back up to the third floor of the hotel she thought about the maid Mr. Okafor had seen. She didn't fit the description of the staff assigned to that floor. Was it possible she didn't work for the hotel at all?

What better way to go about unnoticed than to disguise yourself as a member of the cleaning staff? They were invisible to most of the hotel guests, going in and out of rooms to replace towels or for a hundred other reasons.

The more Abby thought about it, the more sense it made. How else could someone enter her room without being noticed? And the cleaning cart made the perfect hiding place. The thief must have gotten possession of a master key card, stolen her catbird, then secreted it away in the cleaning cart before making an escape.

The most disturbing part of this whole incident was that someone must have deliberately targeted her. This was no random burglary. Someone had broken into her hotel room specifically to steal the painting since none of their other possessions were touched.

Anxiety knotted her stomach. The first person who came into her mind was Marcus. He'd admired her painting and even tried to buy it, though she didn't want to believe he'd actually steal it. If she looked at this objectively, the culprit could be someone connected with the *Antique Adventures* show or even one of the residents of Sparrow Island. They were the only ones who knew about her painting and its possible value. They were also the only ones who knew her room number.

There were other, more remote possibilities like someone targeting her and Mary when they checked into the hotel, but that seemed unlikely. Besides, she couldn't escape the fact that only her painting was taken, not Mary's jewelry or the scrimshaw. The thief had probably been in and out of their room in a matter of minutes.

A headache began to throb in her temple, her body's signal that she needed to eat something. Maybe after lunch her head would stop reeling from this mystery and she'd be able to sort it all out.

When she opened the door to her hotel room, she saw her sister seated in front of the open closet, sorting through the clothes hanging there.

"There you are," Mary exclaimed. "I was beginning to wonder what happened to you."

"Have you ordered lunch yet?" Abby asked her, setting her bag down. "I'm starving."

"Forget about food for now," Mary advised her. "Have I got a surprise for you!"

CHAPTER ❧ ELEVEN

WHAT KIND OF SURPRISE," asked Abby, sincerely wishing she could just kick off her shoes and relax.

"You have a lunch date," Mary announced.

"Yes, with you and Finnegan."

"No, I mean a real date. With a man."

Abby's stomach rumbled and she reached for the mint the maid had left on her pillow this morning. "I have no idea what you're talking about."

"I'm talking about Marcus Wolfe." Mary pulled some clothes from the closet and handed them to Abby. "I think you should wear this outfit. It really complements your brown eyes."

"Mary, wait," Abby implored her. "Please tell me what's going on."

Her sister smiled. "I guess I am getting a little ahead of myself. Marcus called a little while ago and asked you to lunch. Since you weren't here, I took the opportunity to accept for you."

Abby looked at the pale pink jacket and matching silk slacks in her hands. "You did?"

Mary's smile faded. "You don't mind, do you? I thought you liked him."

"I do like him . . ." Her voice trailed off as she wondered about the purpose behind his invitation. Did he want to make her another offer on her catbird painting or was this lunch date more personal?

"I thought you did," Mary said, choosing a pair of shoes for her to wear. "Now you'd better get ready. You don't have much time."

Abby stared at the clothes in her hands. "What if I don't want to go to lunch with Marcus?"

Mary arched a silver brow in disbelief. "You don't want to go to lunch with a handsome, eligible bachelor who seems smitten with you? I'm sorry, Abby, I can't allow it. You deserve to have some fun on this trip. And Marcus has fun written all over him."

Abby couldn't help but smile at her sister's bossy manner. "So I'm to have fun on this trip whether I like it or not?"

Mary laughed. "Yes. We're on vacation, after all. It may have started off a little rocky, what with your catbird being stolen and the mess with Finnegan, but now it's time we turned it around." She checked her watch. "I told Marcus you'd meet him at noon at that fancy French restaurant near the lobby, so we don't have much time to waste."

A thrill of anticipation shot through Abby. This date was completely unexpected, which made it all the more exciting. "I suppose I could go."

"You're going," Mary insisted. "Now sit down here while I help you with your makeup."

Twenty minutes later, Abby walked into the restaurant, her heart skipping in her chest. She looked around, wondering for a moment if Marcus had backed out of their lunch date at the last minute. Then she saw him stand up near a table at the corner and wave to her.

Abby smiled as she headed toward him, pleased that Mary had taken the time to help her with her hair and makeup. Especially since Marcus looked so handsome in his olive green suit, beige dress shirt and black tie.

"We meet again," Marcus said, holding a chair out for her.

Abby took a seat. "Thank you for the lunch invitation. It was a nice surprise."

"I'm just glad you could join me on such short notice. I've been busier than I expected and didn't have a chance to contact you earlier."

A waiter approached their table. "Are you ready to order or would you like a few more minutes?"

Abby opened the menu in front of her, surprised to find it written in French. She glanced up at Marcus. "I may need some time to decipher this."

"I'll be happy to translate for you." He moved his chair closer to hers. "I wish we could order a sample of everything on the menu, just so you could choose a favorite."

She laughed. "Don't tempt me. I saw the dessert cart on the way in and had the same thought."

"Are you in the mood for seafood?" Marcus asked her. "Or perhaps a terrine or fricassee? I've heard they also have wonderful soufflés here."

"Perhaps I'll start with cheese soufflé and end with a chocolate one."

He grinned. "A woman after my own heart."

At last she settled on a salmon and spinach terrine served on a bed of wild rice. The waiter approached their table and Marcus kept his chair next to Abby's as he placed their order in perfect French.

Abby sat back, impressed with his knowledge. She wondered where he had learned French and how often he invited women he'd just met out for lunch.

"Now," he said, reaching for his crystal water glass, "tell me how you like your experience with *Antique Adventures* so far."

She met his gaze, unsettled by the possibility that he could be the thief. "A little too eventful for my taste."

Curiosity lit his handsome face. "In what way?"

"Well, my catbird painting made it on to the show," she began, watching carefully for his reaction, "but someone broke into our hotel room last night while Mary and I were out to dinner and stole it."

His shock seemed genuine. Before she could respond, the waiter approached and set their salad plates in front of them. When he departed, Marcus leaned closer to her and said, "Please tell me you're joking."

"I wish I was," Abby said, relaxing a little. She picked up her salad fork and began eating. "Unfortunately, it's all too true."

"Do the police have any suspects?"

Abby hesitated, poking her fork among the fresh radicchio. "We decided not to call the police. The hotel detective is in charge of the case and I'm helping with the investigation."

Marcus arched a brow. "Are you sure that's wise?"

"I think it was the right decision," Abby told him. "In exchange for not involving the police, which might have resulted in the show changing venues, the hotel is giving me full access to whatever I need to find my painting."

"So what have you discovered so far?"

"Not much, I'm afraid." She explained about Mr. Okafor's calling to complain about Finnegan and his sighting of a hotel maid near her room.

"So it was one of the staff."

Abby shrugged. "I don't think so. His description was so vague and it didn't fit either of the maids assigned to the floor that evening. I'm beginning to think it was someone masquerading as a maid."

"Clever," Marcus said with a thoughtful nod. "No one would find it unusual for a maid to enter your room, even if you weren't there."

"Exactly." Abby took another bite of her salad. "And with a staff of more than one hundred and eighty, it probably wouldn't be too hard to bribe one of them into leaving a uniform and cleaning cart where the thief could have access to it."

Marcus dabbed at his mouth with the white linen napkin. "Finding this thief is going to be quite a challenge."

Abby reached for her water glass. "It will be worth it if I get my catbird back."

"I still think you should at least file a police report, unless . . ." His words trailed off as he looked over at her.

"Unless . . . what?" Abby prodded.

"Unless you suspect someone you know of the theft. Someone from Sparrow Island, perhaps?"

"I considered that," Abby admitted, "but quickly dismissed it as a possibility. I know and trust them. Besides, we were all at dinner together last night when the theft occurred."

Marcus pushed his empty salad plate aside. "I wish there was something I could do to help."

Abby smiled. "This lunch is helping already. I needed a

break and a chance to collect my thoughts. So thank you for the invitation."

"It's my pleasure. In fact, I'm enjoying it so much I wonder if you'd be willing to repeat the experience."

Her heart skipped a beat. What had she done to deserve this kind of attention?

"Will you be my date for the reception tomorrow evening?" Marcus asked her. "*Antique Adventures* puts on quite a party for all its television participants and for antique dealers like me."

She'd read about the reception in the brochure, but hadn't decided if she was going to attend. Mary would probably insist on taking her shopping for a new dress if she accepted.

"Please don't keep me in suspense," Marcus urged as the waiter approached the table to collect their empty salad plates. "Do we have a date?"

Abby threw caution to the wind, intent on enjoying every spare moment of her vacation. "We do."

IN THE MIDDLE of their entrée, Abby looked up to find Marcus staring at her.

"Is something wrong?" she asked.

He smiled. "Not at all. I'm just debating on whether to ask you a favor."

That intrigued her. "What is it?"

"Would you consider going undercover for me?"

She blinked at him. "What?"

He smiled at her reaction. "It's not nearly as ominous as it sounds. I'd simply like you to pose as a potential buyer for an antique. You see, I believe Valerie Lendl, a fellow dealer I've known for quite sometime, is quoting me an inflated price because I'm one of her competitors."

"Oh." Abby dabbed at her mouth with the white linen napkin. "I'm not sure I could pull it off or if I would even want to try. I don't like deceiving people."

"Believe me, Valerie won't mind. She's done the same to me several times. However, I don't want you to do anything that makes you uncomfortable." He leaned across the table, his voice low and his gaze intense. "I do have to disagree about your ability to pull it off. You are an intelligent, fascinating woman, Abby Stanton. I believe you could accomplish anything you set your mind to."

A hot blush rose to her cheeks at his compliment and she decided this was a good time to change the subject. "My terrine is delicious."

Marcus nodded, enjoying his own terrine of pork and truffles. "This was one of my favorite dishes when I lived in Paris. Of course, I was just a poor student then, so I couldn't afford to dine out very often. But when I did, I always ordered it and enjoyed every bite."

"So you went to college in Paris?" Abby asked, eager to learn more about him.

"I studied at a small art school there," he replied. "I wanted to be a famous artist. However, I soon learned that my true talent lay in buying and selling art rather than creating it."

"Which led to your import/export business?"

"Yes. I expanded my company into other areas besides art. But that's always remained my first love, which is the reason why I couldn't resist offering to buy your catbird painting. Something about it appealed to me. I can't even explain it."

She knew exactly what he meant because she'd had the same reaction. It wasn't a perfect painting, yet there was a rawness to it that appealed to her. Something about the colors and the lines made her feel good when she looked at it.

"Here I am," he remarked, "chattering on like a magpie." He picked up his water glass. "Did you know that in China, the magpie symbolizes good fortune?"

"I do," Abby replied. "In other cultures, the magpie is regarded as a thief and not a very popular bird, I'm afraid."

"Quite a dichotomy." Marcus flashed a grin at her, then resumed eating, his dark head bent over his plate.

Abby watched him, the thought suddenly niggling at her that Marcus had the motive, means and opportunity to steal her painting. He'd offered to buy it on the *Victoria Clipper* without even knowing its value.

Yet, as far as she knew, he was unaware of her room number. Abby breathed a sigh of relief, surprised at how much she didn't want Marcus to be the culprit. She'd almost rather never find her catbird at all than discover he was responsible for stealing it.

"You're not eating," he observed. "Is something wrong with the food?"

"No, not at all," she replied, shaking off her suspicions. She wasn't going to let her investigation ruin her lunch date. "It's very rich, though. I doubt I'll be able to finish it."

"Then we must ask the waiter for a doggy bag. Perhaps your sister would enjoy it."

His thoughtfulness touched her. "Thank you. I think I will."

"All the hotel rooms are appointed with a refrigerator and terrines keep very well." He chuckled. "Believe me, I know. I lived on leftovers for several days each time I indulged myself at a fancy Paris restaurant."

The more he talked, the more Abby doubted that Marcus

could be the thief. Besides, why would he ask her out for lunch if he'd stolen from her? He certainly wouldn't encourage her to file a police report.

"I've told you some of my background," Marcus said. "Now it's your turn. How did you become interested in ornithology?"

"It was a gradual process," Abby began, putting her suspicions out of her mind. "Growing up on Sparrow Island, I learned to love the outdoors and all the wildlife. My father owned a charter boat, and I'd spend most of my free time sailing with him. That's when I knew that whatever career I chose for myself, I wouldn't want to be stuck in an office all day."

"Perfectly understandable," Marcus agreed. "That's what I love about the antiques business. I get the chance to traipse around the country to estate sales and events like this on a regular basis."

"I never really thought about a career in ornithology," she said, continuing her story, "until I found an injured robin on our farm."

"And you restored it to health?"

Abby shook her head. "Just the opposite, I'm afraid. Almost as soon as I gathered it up and settled it into a cardboard box to recuperate, it died."

"That's not a very happy ending. How old were you when this happened?"

"Thirteen," Abby replied. "I was traumatized by the event and afraid that I'd done something to hasten its death. So I started researching robins to find out what I'd done wrong."

"Ah," said Marcus, nodding. "And the seed was planted."

She smiled. "Once I started reading about birds, I couldn't seem to stop. They fascinated me. I learned everything there was to know about robins, then moved on to water fowl. It grew from there."

"And a career was born."

"I've been very fortunate," Abby mused. "I knew what I wanted to do with my life early on. So many people flounder for a while, searching for their passion and often taking the wrong road."

"But are there really any wrong roads?" Marcus inquired, echoing the discussion she'd had earlier with her former student. "I believe that there's a reason for each path we take. It's the journey that counts, not the destination."

She stared at him. "That's what I believe too. That God leads us in the right direction if we listen to Him. If we don't, then we have something to learn along the way."

"I knew you were a fascinating woman," Marcus observed. "You just proved me right."

Abby wondered if she was headed in the right direction with Marcus. She liked him, but she really knew nothing about him.

"What do you have planned for the rest of the day?" he asked her.

She set her napkin next to her plate. "I'm having my grandmother's locket evaluated this afternoon, then meeting with my boss, Hugo Baron, this evening.

"I see." He captured her gaze. "Is that all he is to you? A boss?"

Abby was taken aback by the question. Was that a flash of jealousy she saw in his eyes? "No. He's also a very good friend."

Marcus smiled. "As I hope to be."

His words warmed Abby's heart. She enjoyed his company and looked forward to their second date tomorrow evening. Despite her vacation's rocky start, she found herself enjoying this surprising flirtation.

CHAPTER ❦ TWELVE

Later that afternoon, Abby sat in the Tamarack Room while the jewelry appraiser carefully studied the old gold locket on the black velvet pad in front of her. Under the bright light, Abby could see all the tiny scratches and blemishes that time had etched into the surface of the precious keepsake.

The appraiser, who had introduced herself as Sylvia Pierce when Abby first sat down, didn't say a word as she studied the locket under a magnifying glass. Sylvia wore a dark purple caftan and just the barest touch of makeup. The sparkling vintage diamonds in her ears and around her throat bespoke a woman who knew fine jewelry.

"I realize it's probably of little value," Abby said as Sylvia pursed her lips. "I'm most interested in any history you might have about it."

"*Sshh*," the appraiser admonished her.

A long line of people waited behind her and Abby could hear them shuffling impatiently as they waited their turn.

Sylvia liked to take her time with each item and Abby herself had waited over an hour, despite Jeffrey giving her one of the lower numbers.

She'd stopped in her hotel room after her lunch with Marcus and found her sister and Finnegan both napping. The room was cool, so she'd covered Mary with a blanket, then hurried down to the Tamarack Room, not even taking time to change out of her pink silk suit.

Just like yesterday, Abby kept having the sense that she was always running behind schedule. So far, this wasn't exactly the relaxing vacation she'd envisioned for so many weeks.

Sylvia turned the locket over, then picked up the magnifying glass once more and leaned so close to the table that her long nose almost brushed the black velvet.

Abby watched her, wondering what exactly she was examining. She'd half expected the appraiser to take one look at the locket and announce that it was of cheap material and mass-produced, giving her no way of tracing its history.

Then again, Abby knew from observing Sylvia with other participants during the hour she'd spent in the waiting line that the appraiser took about the same amount of time with each item, no matter what its value.

The one advantage to the long wait was the opportunity to observe so many interesting items. She'd seen antiques spanning five centuries from all over the world.

"Black," Sylvia proclaimed at last, her voice a bit hoarse from not speaking for so long. She cleared it, then carefully replaced the necklace on the velvet pad.

Abby looked around her, wondering if she was supposed to know what that meant. Perhaps it was a code word for a member of the crew to bring up the next item. She heard more shuffling behind her and someone complaining about how long the evaluation process was taking.

"Do you know him?" Sylvia asked, looking up at Abby.

"Know who?" she asked, looking around her.

"Nigel Black," the appraiser clarified. "He was a goldsmith who immigrated to New York from Great Britain in the late nineteenth century."

"You mean Mr. Black made this locket?"

"Indeed." She pointed to the back of the locket. "His mark is barely visible to the naked eye, but quite clear with a magnifying glass."

Abby couldn't see anything, but she took the expert's word for it. "So this was made in New York?"

The appraiser nodded. "No later than the turn of the century, as Mr. Black died of a sudden apoplexy in 1905. Apoplexy, of course, was the word used to describe a stroke or brain hemorrhage back in those days. Now we use much more complicated terms to describe the same thing, like cerebral infarction."

Someone groaned behind Abby and she knew why. Earlier, Sylvia had given a fifteen minute lecture on the science of grafting olive trees to a man who had brought a pearl bracelet to be appraised. She seemed to have a little difficulty staying on topic.

Sylvia sat back in her chair, smiling like a cat who had just found a bowl of cream. "What can you tell me about this locket?"

"Not much," Abby admitted. She explained her grandmother's journey on the orphan train and how the locket was one of the few possessions that had come with her on the trip.

"Were your grandmother's parents wealthy?" Sylvia asked her.

"I'm almost certain they were not." Abby thought about Grandma Lora's mother giving her up in the hopes of finding a better life for her daughter. "I believe they were very poor."

The appraiser arched a brow. "So you don't know where your grandmother got the locket?"

Abby shook her head. "I don't know anything about it, that's why I brought the locket to you."

"Tell me something," the appraiser said. "How old was your grandmother when she left New York City on the orphan train."

"Eleven."

Sylvia nodded. "Old enough, then."

"Old enough for what?"

Sylvia smiled at her. "We'll wait to reveal that when we do the taping."

Abby blinked in surprise. "You mean you want to have the locket on the show?"

"Oh, most definitely. I believe it will be one of our most interesting segments ever."

Now Abby was intrigued. Did the locket have more value than she'd imagined or, even better, would Sylvia be able to tell her something about its history that would provide insight into her grandmother's early life before heading to Nebraska?

It saddened her a little to think that Grandma Lora might have held the key to allow her to stay with her mother. If the locket was valuable and they'd sold it . . . Abby shook that speculation from her mind. She couldn't turn back the clock or play the "what if" game. The past had already been written.

But not the future. She hoped whatever story the locket had to tell would be a blessing for her mother.

A mischievous gleam twinkled in the appraiser's eyes. "I think you'll be quite surprised at what I have to tell you. In fact, it's simply amazing to me that your grandmother never sold it, given her situation."

That confirmed for Abby that the locket was worth a lot of money, though Sylvia hadn't actually come out and said it.

Abby and Mary and their mother had always assumed the locket simply had sentimental value for Grandma Lora. She was the least likely person to ever wear fancy jewelry, refusing to spend her money on such fripperies, as she called them.

"Hans," Sylvia called to her assistant. "We need to schedule this lady for taping. Be sure and build in some extra time for this one so we can approach it from the orphan train angle and go from there."

The young man hurried over to Abby to take down her information, his quickness and efficiency almost the polar opposite of the appraiser he assisted. If she recalled correctly, this was the philosophy major that Jeffrey had told her about.

"We'll need you here at ten o'clock sharp on Thursday morning," he said, checking the schedule printed on his clipboard.

Abby started filling out information on the release form. "This asks for the name and address of the item's owner. The locket actually belongs to my mother, so should I put my name or hers?"

"Go ahead and put her name and address," Hans told her. "We might decide to put photos of the locket on our Web site and would need to obtain permission from the owner to do that."

Abby followed his instructions, then handed the papers back to him. "Is that all you need?"

"That should do it," Hans replied.

She wondered whether to mention the conflict with her scheduled taping of the catbird painting since it had been stolen, then decided to be optimistic that she'd have it back by then.

"I'm supposed to be here at ten o'clock on Thursday for another taping with Dr. Houston," she told Hans as he sorted through his file folder.

"I'll move your taping to an afternoon slot," he promised. "Chances are he'll be running behind anyway since no one around here can seem to stick to a schedule." He shook his head in disgust. "Does time have meaning or does meaning have time? It's the eternal question I keep asking myself."

Abby bit back a smile at his obscure philosophical musing. "Is that all you need from me?"

"Just your signature right here, please," he said, pointing to the dotted line at the bottom of the page.

It was the same contractual agreement Abby had signed for Chloe that released the show from any responsibility for her antique getting damaged during the taping.

Abby signed it, then handed the pen back to Sylvia's crew assistant.

"We'll see you on Thursday, Dr. Stanton." Then Hans turned to the line behind her and shouted, "Next! Come on, people, let's move it. We've got a television show to produce here."

As Abby left the conference room, she still couldn't believe they wanted her to appear on the show with Grandma Lora's locket. She had to admit to herself that she was a little apprehensive about what they were going to tell her. The expression she'd seen on Sylvia's face unsettled her for some reason.

Except for the tidbit about the lock of hair that Grandma Lora had revealed to Mary, no one in her family knew much about those early years. Ellen had surmised that her mother's family had even been homeless at one time from one of the few comments that Grandma Lora had ever made.

Now Abby wondered why their family hadn't at least tried to sell the locket to afford the basic necessities of food and shelter.

It was a question that might never be answered. Abby carefully placed the locket back in her purse. At least now she knew the name of the goldsmith who had made the locket and it seemed apparent she'd find out even more about it during the taping of the show on Thursday.

Or maybe she didn't have to wait that long.

Abby turned around and headed toward the hotel business office on the main level. The spacious room allowed its guests to have access to a copy machine, a fax machine, typewriters, and best of all, a bank of computers with Internet access.

All but one of the computers was in use when she got there. She sat down in the empty chair, placing her bag on the counter beside her. Then she turned on the computer and waited for the machine to power up. When it did, she clicked on the Internet icon and connected to her favorite search engine.

"Nigel Black," she murmured under her breath as she typed his name into the box on the screen. It took a few seconds for the results to appear.

When they did, Abby sat up in the chair, feeling as if she couldn't catch her breath. There, on the fourth link on the page, was a picture of her grandmother's locket.

Abby clicked on the link, then waited as an even larger picture of the locket downloaded onto the screen. It looked like a very old photograph of the same locket that was now in her purse. Then she turned her attention to the text.

What she read there made her gasp out loud.

"Hey, Dr. Stanton!"

Abby quickly closed the window on the computer before anyone could see it. Then she looked up to find Jeffrey waving to her on the other side of the glass wall.

His friend Chloe stood beside him holding a clipboard. She had an ink mark on her cheek and her hands looked like she'd been trying to remove dark red fingernail polish that had bled into her cuticles.

Abby waved to the two of them, her heart still pounding from what she'd just read. Picking up her bag, she joined Jeffrey and Chloe out in the lobby.

"Hey, I was hoping to run into you today," Jeffrey said. "Are you free for a late lunch?"

"I'm sorry," Abby replied. "I've already eaten."

"Then how about some dessert?" he countered. "It's all free. The hotel sets up a big buffet backstage for the crew every day. You can come as my guest."

Abby smiled at the thought of receiving two lunch invitations from two handsome, single men on the same day. Although Jeffrey was young enough to be her son, she was still flattered that he wanted to spend time with her.

"I might tag along," Abby said, "if you're sure you don't mind."

"Not at all," he replied. "Chloe probably gets tired of my company. It'll be nice to talk to someone about birds who's as interested in them as I am."

"The crew nicknamed him Tweety," Chloe quipped, "because all he ever talks about is birds. I've learned more about ornithology in the last couple of years than I ever imagined possible."

"You're exaggerating just a little," Jeffrey said as they walked toward the ballroom. "But I'll admit I do get carried away sometimes. That's easy to do, isn't it, Dr. Stanton?"

Abby smiled, falling easily into step with the two of them. "I could talk about birds all day long," she admitted, "although I usually try to restrain myself when I'm not working."

"Wonderful," Chloe exclaimed. "Then let's agree to a bird-free conversation for lunch."

"Deal," Jeffrey replied. "But only if Dr. Stanton and I can get together later to talk about birds."

"I'm free for lunch tomorrow," Abby told him. "Would that work for you?"

He frowned. "I'm afraid not. In fact, I think I'm pretty busy for the rest of the week. Things get pretty crazy around here when we start taping."

Abby couldn't imagine anything more chaotic than what she'd witnessed during the last two days. She'd watch the show with an entirely new appreciation after this week was over.

"Hey, do you happen to have my schedule with you?" Jeffrey asked Chloe.

She consulted the clipboard in her hands. "Tomorrow is Wednesday and you're booked solid. Same with Thursday. Friday morning we pack up and fly to Toronto for the next show.

He sighed. "That figures. The one chance I have to talk with another bird enthusiast and I've got no time to do it."

When they reached the backstage area Abby saw a long table filled with assorted sandwiches, chips, sodas and an array of finger desserts.

"Hold on just a minute," Chloe said, flipping through the scheduling sheets on her clipboard. "It looks like you have about half an hour free on Thursday around noon. It must be some kind of miracle."

He brightened. "Hey, maybe we can meet up for a quick bite to eat. Does that time work for you, Dr. Stanton?"

"I think so," Abby replied. "My taping is scheduled for ten o'clock."

"Perfect," Jeffrey exclaimed. "As long as Ned doesn't start playing perfectionist during the tapings, then I should be able to make it."

"Did I hear someone call my name?" a deep voice intoned behind them.

They all turned around and Jeffrey made the introductions.

"Dr. Stanton, this is Ned Brinkman, our ace camera man and Hans Turner, the show's scheduling whiz. They're an integral part of making sure *Antique Adventures* runs smoothly."

"Okay, Kugler," Ned said warily. "What's with all the compliments? You want something from us, don't you?"

Jeffrey grinned. "Just make sure we're done with the morning taping in time for me to make it to lunch at noon on Thursday, okay?"

"Noon!" Hans exclaimed, his face filled with horror. "We're supposed to be done taping at eleven. If we start running an hour behind like we did back in Phoenix I'm going to quit my job on the spot."

Abby saw them all look over at Ned.

"Hey, it's not my fault," he protested. "Somebody messed with my camera and I had to get it working properly if I didn't want to be fired."

"Well, don't let anybody mess with it this time," Jeffrey

warned him. "I could really use that thirty-minute break this week."

"Jeff wants to talk to Dr. Stanton about birds," Chloe informed the other two.

Hans sighed. "Better you than us, Dr. Stanton."

Abby joined Jeffrey and Chloe at the buffet table, helping herself to a miniature chocolate éclair while the other two piled their plates high with sandwiches and chips.

When they were seated, Jeffrey turned to Abby. "So are you having fun at the show so far?"

She pondered the question for a moment. "I'm not sure that's exactly the word I'd use. Have you heard about my bird painting?"

He picked up his ham sandwich, the meat and cheese bulging out of the bread. "No, what about it?"

"Someone broke into my hotel room last evening and stole it."

"Not again," Ned moaned.

Abby looked up at him in surprise. "Again? You mean it's happened before."

"At almost every show we tape," Jeffrey said with a sigh. "The good news is that the item is usually returned right before the segment is to be taped. The bad news is that the prankster has never been caught."

Abby took a moment to digest her éclair and this new information. In the Bristol Hotel's urgency to keep the theft of her painting a secret from the people in charge of the *Antique Adventures* show, they'd missed the opportunity to discover that this was a routine occurrence.

"I still think it's old Houston," Hans said. "He's been wanting to shake things up ever since the show tried to force him to retire a year ago. That's when things started disappearing. And did you notice most of the thefts are in the category he appraises?"

"Well, the show's done a good job of keeping it quiet if it is him," Chloe said. "They don't want the word getting out that there's a thief among one of their prime-time players."

Abby was fascinated to hear the inside information of the show. She'd never have guessed from watching it on television that Dr. Houston was a disgruntled employee or that a series of odd thefts had plagued the show.

"I still say it's some kind of prank," Jeffrey countered. "Most of the items taken are returned in as good a shape as they were before."

"Most, but not all," Chloe reminded him. "Some are never seen again."

"Is it horrible to wish that some of the antiques are stolen before we see them?" Hans asked. "We had a lady yesterday who brought in an old tin plate she'd found buried in the dirt floor of an old hog building. She hadn't even bothered to clean it off and it was covered with more than just dirt, if you know what I mean."

Chloe wrinkled her nose. "Please Hans, some of us are trying to eat here."

"Sorry," he said, then turned to Abby. "The point is that you don't need to worry about it. Your painting will probably show up in time for you to appear on the show with it."

The fact that the four of them saw the theft as a prank didn't deter Abby from wanting to find the culprit. Whoever had taken her painting had also harmed Finnegan in the process. She didn't regard locking a sick dog in a dark closet as a prank.

"How often has this happened?" she asked them.

Jeffrey shrugged. "In almost every city for the last ten months or so. The show keeps revamping security and demanding that each hotel have a detective on staff, but it doesn't seem to help."

"We've all had background checks done on us," Chloe commented, "and now all the employees of the show are bonded by a surety company."

Ned licked a dab of frosting off his fingertip. "That's one of the reasons the release form we have everyone sign makes it clear that *Antique Adventures* takes no responsibility for lost, stolen or missing items."

"With an emphasis on stolen," Jeffrey said wryly. "Although borrowed might be the more appropriate word since they're usually returned."

That only made the mystery more interesting to Abby. Did the thief just steal for the thrill of it? To prove it could be done or to highlight the lax security on the show? Whatever the reason, there was absolutely no excuse for invading her privacy by breaking into her hotel room or for shoving Finnegan into the closet.

"Well, we'd better get back to work," Jeffrey said, brushing the crumbs off his hands. "I'll see you on Thursday."

"I'm looking forward to it."

Chloe consulted her clipboard again. "You might want to stick around and wait for him if he doesn't show up at noon right away. There's a good chance we'll be running late no matter what Hans says."

"That will give me a chance to people-watch," Abby replied, "and that's one of my favorite hobbies."

He grinned. "Along with bird-watching?"

Chloe groaned. "Please, you promised no bird talk."

Jeffrey rolled his eyes at her, then waved good-bye to Abby. "See you later, Dr. Stanton."

She watched the four of them walk off, wondering if one of them knew more than they were telling. Since they thought of the incidents as harmless pranks, they might be reluctant to finger the culprit.

All the more reason she'd have to find the thief herself.

CHAPTER ❦ THIRTEEN

Before Abby knew it, Tuesday evening had arrived and she still hadn't met with Bill Briley. She'd checked in with the front desk several times during the day, but they were just as perplexed by his absence.

She'd spent the rest of the afternoon doing more research on the locket and had developed a slight headache from the glare of the computer screen. As she emerged from the business office, Hugo hailed her from the lobby. They were due to meet in fifteen minutes for a museum tour and Abby still wanted to change her clothes.

"There you are," he said, hurrying over to her. "I've been looking everywhere for you."

"I've been doing some research," she replied, hoping he didn't ask her to elaborate. "If you just give me a few minutes, I'll be ready to go."

"It's not that," he said, his expression growing somber.

"I don't think we're going to have time to make it to the museum tonight. Something's happened."

Fear clutched her. "What is it? Is Mary all right? Or is it Finnegan?"

"No, nothing like that," he assured her. "They're both fine."

Abby breathed a sigh of relief as Hugo placed his palm on her elbow and guided her toward the elevator.

"I'm afraid we have another problem, though. Thelma wants to see you immediately."

"What happened?" Abby asked. "Did she and her sister have another fight?"

"I promised to let her explain it all." He pushed the button for Thelma's floor, then turned to look at her. "I meant to tell you earlier that you look very nice today, Abby. That color is very flattering on you."

A blush crept up her cheeks. "Thank you."

More people entered the elevator, effectively ending their conversation. As they rode up to the seventh floor, Abby wondered what had happened. She hoped Betty hadn't gone back to Florida, especially since Thelma had made the effort to invite her to Seattle and had even given her that treasured family photograph.

By the time they reached Thelma's room, most of the Sparrow Island group was already there. Thelma sat on the edge of the king-size bed. Mary sat in her wheelchair beside the older woman, gently patting her narrow shoulder.

"I can't believe it," Thelma muttered, dabbing at her eyes with a tissue. "I just can't believe it."

Abby followed Hugo into the room. "What happened, Thelma? Hugo said you wanted to see me."

Thelma looked up at her, tears welling in her eyes. "You're the only one who can truly understand, Abby. Someone stole my mother's teapot."

"What?" Abby exclaimed, never expecting to hear something like this.

"It's true," Thelma said with a sniff. "The same hooligans that took your painting made off with Mama's teapot while Betty and I were enjoying a late lunch." Her face twisted with anger. "If I ever get my hands on the dirty, rotten—"

"Whoa," Abby admonished, moving closer to Thelma. "Calm down. In fact, why don't you tell me your story from the beginning?"

Naomi handed Thelma a cup of tea. "Be careful, it's hot."

"Thank you." Thelma took the cup from her. "The doctor said I shouldn't let myself get worked up like this. It's not good for my blood pressure. It was just such a shock to come back from our lunch and find Betty's room ransacked like that. The poor girl is so distraught she had to take a tranquilizer. She said it was worse than the hurricane she lived through two years ago when her house was almost destroyed."

Abby looked around the hotel room, realizing that Thelma's sister wasn't among the crowd.

"The security in this place is ridiculous," Joe said. "That makes two thefts in two days."

"Now I know why I rarely leave Sparrow Island," Lindsey mused. "It's just not safe anywhere else."

Everyone began talking at once. Abby watched Thelma sip her tea and sensed that the woman was beginning to calm down a little.

"How long were you at lunch with your sister?" Abby asked.

Thelma didn't hesitate. "About an hour and a half.

I checked because I always take my blood pressure pill at five o'clock and we didn't get to the restaurant until a little after three. I was worried I wouldn't make it back to my room in time, but we did."

Abby thought about the time, realizing she'd been enjoying the company of Jeffrey and his friends while the thief had broken into Betty's room and stolen the teapot.

"Then you both went to Betty's room?"

Thelma nodded. "It's on the sixth floor. We knew as soon as we walked in the door that something had happened." She paused to take another sip of her tea. "The bed covers were strewn all over, along with the clothes from her suitcase. But the only thing missing was Mama's beautiful teapot."

"That's just awful," Lindsey muttered. "Who would do such a thing?"

"I have no idea." Thelma's mouth tightened. "But I'm going to see to it that these criminals are prosecuted to the furthest extent of the law!"

"Criminals?" Abby echoed. "What makes you think it was more than one?"

Thelma hesitated. "I don't know. I guess I just assumed it when I talked to Mr. Briley."

Abby was confused. "The hotel detective?"

"That's him," Thelma looked surprised that Abby would even have to ask. "He interviewed me this morning about the theft of your bird painting. He was very thorough and wanted all the details I could give him. It's a good thing I had those notes from our group interview on the *Victoria Clipper*."

"He interviewed me too," Naomi volunteered. "I think he intends to talk to all of us sooner or later."

"That's what he told me too." Joe looked around the room.

"He's kind of an interesting fellow. Had lots of stories about his time on the police force."

Abby looked at her sister. "Have you talked to him, Mary?"

"No, I haven't," she replied. "Finnegan and I have been in the room most of the day. It's rather strange he didn't call us, isn't it?"

Abby had to agree. She assumed a professional investigator would speak to the victims of the crime before anyone else.

A frown worried Hugo's expression. "When I allowed Mr. Briley to interview me, he indicated that he'd already spoken to both of you. Otherwise, I would have insisted that he meet with you first to get all the facts."

"What time did you see him?" Abby asked.

"Around four o'clock. He said that he'd be finished working for the day as soon as he wrapped up his interview with me."

"Then I'll have to meet with Mr. Briley tomorrow to get it all straightened out."

She had every intention of tracking down the hotel detective first thing in the morning and comparing notes, especially now that she knew this kind of thing had happened at other venues of the *Antique Adventures* show. It seemed pretty clear to her that the thief was someone on the crew.

"What about my teapot?" Thelma moaned. "How are we going to find it in time to appear on the show?"

Abby almost said that the teapot might show up again, but what if it was one of the few items that wasn't returned?

"I'd like to talk to Betty as soon as possible," Abby told her. "Do you have any idea when she'll be feeling better?"

Thelma sighed. "The poor thing was already exhausted from her trip before this happened. Maybe after a good night's sleep she'll be composed enough to talk to you about it."

Tears welled up again in Thelma's eyes. "I can't believe Mama's teapot might really be gone forever. How could something like this happen?"

Abby wished she knew the answer to that question. She'd been asking it herself since last night. She reached out to pat her hand. "I'm so sorry, Thelma."

"Thank you." Thelma dabbed at her eyes again. "Let this be a warning for all of you to barricade your doors tonight. Who knows what that sneaky thief will try to steal next?"

Abby wondered how the thief even knew about the teapot or how to find Betty's room. Of course, Thelma had talked about it to everyone she met, including the appraiser at the preliminary evaluation. It would be easy enough for someone to loiter in the front lobby and overhear Betty's room number when she checked in this morning.

The group began to disperse and Thelma agreed to take a walk around the hotel with Naomi to clear her head.

Abby knew she'd have a better understanding of the situation when she finally talked to Betty tomorrow. There might be things the woman could tell her that Thelma had inadvertently left out.

Her first order of business tomorrow was to track down Bill Briley and make it clear that she was an equal partner in this investigation.

CHAPTER ❦ FOURTEEN

ON WEDNESDAY MORNING, Abby found the hotel detective eating a huge oatmeal raisin cookie in his office. There were crumbs all over the green ink blotter on his desk and even some on his tie.

"Come in," he called out when he saw her standing in the open doorway. "Dr. Stanton, I presume?"

Bill Briley's blue suit looked one size too small for his rotund frame and an old-fashioned brown mustache curled over his upper lip. He looked to be in his late fifties, and she noticed several commendation plaques hung on the wall behind him.

She walked inside the office. "How did you know who I am?"

He grinned. "I saw your picture during the background check."

"You conducted a background check?" Abby echoed. "On me?"

"Of course," he replied, brushing cookie crumbs off his striped tie. "One of my rules of investigation is to clear the so-called victims first. Saves a lot of wasted time."

He leaned back in his brown leather office chair and folded his arms behind his head. "You'd be amazed at how many people try to hide their own crimes by pretending to be the hapless victim of someone else. Saw it many times when I was on the force."

She'd only known the man for thirty seconds and he already rubbed her the wrong way. Still, he was investigating her case, and they'd have to learn to work together.

"I assure you that I didn't steal my own catbird painting," Abby told him. She took a seat on the metal folding chair opposite the desk. The less than comfortable furnishings made it clear that Briley didn't care about making his visitors feel welcome.

"Oh, I know that," he replied. "I run background checks for other reasons too. It makes it easier for me when I take a witness statement if I know a little about the person I'm interviewing."

Abby supposed that made sense, although she still didn't like the idea of the hotel detective digging into her background without her knowledge. "So what did you find out about me?"

He pulled a file from the stack on his desk and opened it. "Fifty-five-year-old spinster. Works as an ornithologist on Sparrow Island. Lives with her widowed sister."

Abby bristled at his use of the word *spinster*. She certainly didn't see herself that way.

"Look," Briley said, scooting his chair closer to the desk, "the manager told me you want in on this investigation, but I'm a professional. I don't want anyone mucking up the works while I'm in the process of solving the case."

Abby closed her eyes and prayed for patience. Then she

opened them again and forced a smile. "I won't muck up your case, Mr. Briley. In fact, I think I can help you, since I've already started an investigation of my own.

He gave her a condescending smile. "I appreciate the offer, but—"

"I talked to a witness," she interjected.

He furrowed his bushy brow. "What witness? Nobody told me about a witness."

"It was a man who saw a maid near my room during the theft. He gave me her description and said she was pushing a cleaning cart. Seems like that would make a perfect hiding place for my picture, wouldn't it?"

He pulled a legal pad toward him and picked up a pencil. "And the name of this witness?"

"Mr. Okafor."

"Address?"

"I don't know, but he was on his way to Japan, so I'm sure it's almost impossible to reach him now."

Briley dropped the pencil. "Fat lot of good that does us now."

Us. Well, that was progress.

Abby wasn't any more eager to work with the brusque detective than he was to work with her, but they'd be able to accomplish a lot more if they at least compared notes along the way.

"So what did this Okafor fellow have to say?" Briley asked her.

Abby relayed Okafor's generic description of the maid and the fact that Mrs. Gable had rules against her staff wearing their hair loose.

"So it could be one of almost two hundred people," he said, shaking his head. "Impossible."

"Or it could be someone who was disguised as a maid," Abby countered. "Someone who has been in enough hotels to understand how things work. All they'd have to do is nab one of those cleaning carts that are always standing in the hallways and have a maid's uniform handy."

He considered that scenario. "And get their hands on one of those master key cards always floating around. I don't care what the hotel says, I know they don't keep as good an eye on them as they claim."

She wasn't about to argue with him now that he actually seemed to be listening to her. "So all we have to do now is comprise a list of suspects—"

"I've already done it," he interjected. "I've also determined that the thief has to be somebody from your hometown."

She stared at him in disbelief. "Someone from Sparrow Island?"

"Yep." He gave her another condescending smile. "Look, Dr. Stanton, I believe whoever stole that painting had to know the location of your room and what was inside that closet. Can you name anyone else who had that kind of information besides these friends of yours?"

As a matter of fact, she could. Marcus Wolfe, though she didn't consider him a suspect, and anyone connected to the *Antique Adventures* show. She'd had to give them her room number in case they needed to contact her. "I can think of several people, actually."

"Like who?"

She told him, but noticed he wasn't writing anything down. "Doesn't this interest you?"

"Very much," he said, then grinned. "But I've got a mind like a steel trap."

Abby sensed he was humoring her, but she continued anyway. "I also think you should know that there's been another theft reported."

His gray eyes narrowed. "Reported by whom?"

"Thelma Rogers and her sister, Betty Carstens. Betty arrived here from Florida yesterday. Thelma met her for a late lunch that afternoon and when they returned to Betty's room they found their family heirloom missing."

"Another painting?" Briley inquired.

"No, a teapot. It was part of a set that belonged to Thelma and Betty's mother. According to Thelma it was quite valuable."

"Oh yes," he mused, looking thoughtful. "I think I remember her talking about it when I interviewed her yesterday morning. In fact, if I recall correctly, that was all the woman talked about. It's hardly a surprise to find out somebody stole the thing if she was blabbing about it all over the hotel."

Abby didn't believe in blaming the victim. "Thelma and Betty are both very upset about the theft. There were differences between the two crimes, though. Betty's room was in shambles, but my room looked exactly the same as we'd left it that evening."

"Except for the missing painting."

"And the missing dog," she explained.

"Right. Eames told me about that mess." He shook his head. "Too bad that dog couldn't have chomped down on the thief instead of the assistant manager. Then neither one of us would have to worry about this case."

Abby was growing more worried by the moment. Mr. Briley didn't impress her at all. She wondered if he always had this kind of abrasive attitude or if he just didn't believe a bird painting and a teapot were worth his attention.

He steepled his fingers under his chin. "So another theft and another connection to Sparrow Island. More than a coincidence, don't you think?"

Abby knew how it looked, but she needed to set him straight. "Everyone from Sparrow Island was with me at dinner Monday evening when my painting was stolen, so they all have solid alibis."

Briley consulted the notepad on his desk. "According to my interview with Hugo Baron, you and your sister Mary stayed to have coffee with him after the others had already left the restaurant."

"Yes, but that was only for a short while. Certainly not long enough for anyone to break into our room, lock Finnegan in the closet and steal the painting."

"It's still a window of opportunity."

She suppressed a sigh of exasperation. "I know everyone here from Sparrow Island and I can vouch for them all. You won't find the thief among them."

Briley pushed his chair back and stood up. "No offense, Dr. Stanton, but I've been in this profession a long time and I can't count how many times I've heard that exact same sentiment. The nice, quiet neighbor who nobody would suspect in a million years is usually the prime candidate in a case like this."

"But why would anyone steal my painting when it may not be worth anything?" Abby inquired. "The only person who knows its worth is the appraiser, Dr. Houston, and I doubt he told anyone from Sparrow Island. That's why it makes more sense to me that the culprit is someone connected to *Antique Adventures.*"

Briley rounded the desk. "Trust me, Dr. Stanton, I know

what I'm doing. In fact, I believe I'm on the brink of solving this case."

She rose to her feet. "You are?"

"That's right." He walked to the door and held it open for her. "All you have to do is follow my lead."

"Where are we going?" Abby asked as they emerged from his office.

"We're going to get your catbird back."

CHAPTER ✿ FIFTEEN

ABBY'S STOMACH SANK when she saw the number on the hotel room door. "This is a mistake."

Briley ignored her and knocked loudly against the wood. She breathed a sigh of relief when there was no answer, but Briley just knocked again, harder the second time.

A few moments later, the door opened and Joe Blackstock stood on the other side.

He smiled when he saw Abby. "Sorry it took me so long. I was on the phone with Margaret."

"We need to talk to you, Mr. Blackstock," Briley announced, striding into his room without so much as an invitation.

"Come on in," Joe told Abby, opening the door wider for her. Then he turned to Briley. "And let's not stand on ceremony. I told you yesterday that you can just call me Joe."

"All right, Joe." Briley glanced around his hotel room. "I hope we haven't caught you at a bad time."

"Not at all. Do you want to conduct a second interview or something?"

"Or something," Bill said wryly. "I'd just like to ask you a few more questions to clear some things up."

"I don't mind at all," Joe said cordially. "Can I get you two something to drink? I think I have a couple of sodas in this little refrigerator here."

"No, thank you," Abby replied. "I'm fine."

Briley nodded his head. "Sure, I'll take one. Got any root beer?"

Joe opened the refrigerator. "Sorry, just cola."

"That'll do," the hotel detective said.

Abby didn't trust Briley and wished he would have conferred with her before barging in on Joe. She was sure she still hadn't convinced him that no one from Sparrow Island could be guilty of theft.

Joe pulled out the other chair. "Go ahead and have a seat here, Abby. I need to stretch my legs for a while anyhow. I'm not used to sitting around this much."

Abby took the seat, wondering what they were doing here. Briley didn't seem to be in any hurry to come to the point as he popped open his soda can.

Joe looked between the two of them. "I'm glad to see you two working together. Abby's quite good at solving mysteries."

"That's what I hear," Briley replied, tipping the can up to his mouth and taking a long drink.

Joe walked over to the window. "Have you spent much time outside of the hotel yet, Abby?

"Not at all," she replied. "So far my vacation hasn't been very relaxing. Hugo and I were supposed to tour a museum yesterday, but then we got called to Thelma's room after the teapot was stolen."

Joe nodded. "That was a shame, wasn't it? Do you think the two thefts are connected?"

"Definitely," Briley interjected.

"Margaret got a call from one of Thelma's friends this morning, so she already knew all about." He grinned. "I guess a person can call home to Sparrow Island to get the news in Seattle."

Briley glanced at Abby, then back at Joe. "I take it you don't keep many secrets from each other on Sparrow Island?"

"No," Joe replied easily. "We all get along pretty well."

Briley pulled his notepad out of his pocket. "Well, we don't want to waste any more of your time, Joe. Let's get down to my questions."

Joe perched himself on the corner of the bed. "Go right ahead."

Briley pulled a pair of bifocals out of his shirt pocket. "Can you tell me what you were doing yesterday afternoon when the teapot was stolen."

"Well, let's see," Joe began. "I was just walking for about an hour around downtown Seattle taking in the sights."

"By yourself?"

Joe nodded. "I like to do that when I go on vacation. Gives me a better feel for the place."

"So there were no witnesses on this walk of yours."

Joe's brow furrowed as he stared at the detective. "There were hundreds of people on the streets, but I don't know any of them."

"Go on."

"What do you mean?"

"Tell us what you did next, Joe, after you came back from this long walk."

"I came back to my room," he said simply.

"Are there any witnesses to that fact?" Briley asked him.

Joe glanced warily at Abby. "No."

"So at the time of this latest theft," Briley summarized, "you were alone and have no one who can account for your whereabouts?"

Joe looked at Abby, then back at Briley again. "Are you two accusing me of being the thief?"

"Of course not," Abby declared. "I know you could never do such a thing."

Briley pursed his lips. "Is she right about that, Joe? Could you ever do such a thing?"

Joe's kind face darkened. "I didn't steal that catbird painting or that teapot. You're completely crazy if you think otherwise."

"That doesn't answer my question." Briley flipped the notepad closed and slipped it back into his shirt pocket along with his bifocals. "Dr. Stanton doesn't think you could ever steal anything. That you're an honest man. Is she right about that?"

"Of course," Joe sputtered.

Briley shook his head. "You shouldn't lie, Joe. Especially to a former policeman. It just doesn't look good."

Abby stood up, tired of Briley's bullying tactics. "I think it's time for us to leave."

"I think that's a good idea," Joe said, walking toward the door.

Briley stayed in his chair. "I'm not going anywhere yet. Not when you've lied to me twice, Joe."

He looked in bewilderment at the hotel detective. "I have no idea what you're talking about."

"Don't you?"

Joe shook his head, then looked to Abby for guidance. "Do you know what he's talking about? Because I'm totally baffled by all of this."

"No, I don't," she said bluntly. "I think you're way out of line, Mr. Briley."

Briley heaved a long sigh. "Then let me clarify. Joe wasn't telling the truth when he said the people on Sparrow Island have no secrets. And he lied by default when he wouldn't answer my question about whether he was capable of theft."

Joe threw his hands up in the air. "I don't know what you're trying to imply."

"I'm not implying anything," Briley countered. "I only deal in facts. And the simple fact is that you have a criminal record. Something I'd bet money that the good folks of Sparrow Island don't know about you."

All the blood drained from Joe's face. "You had to go back a long time to find out about that, didn't you, Briley?"

The detective nodded. "Thanks to the wonders of cyberspace, it doesn't take much effort to dig up information about someone in newspaper archives or an old police file."

"What are you talking about?" Abby asked, looking between the two of them.

Briley turned to her. "Now do you see, Dr. Stanton, why it takes a professional for this job? A thorough background check revealed that your friend here has a history with theft. Isn't that right, Joe?"

Joe turned to her. "Is that why you brought him to my room, Abby? To accuse me of taking your painting and Betty's teapot?"

"Of course not, Joe," Abby protested. "I had no idea he was going to say—"

"That I'm a thief?" Joe finished for her. He raked a hand through his hair. "Well, it's the truth, I guess. Although I never realized they even kept police records that far back."

Briley smiled, clearly enjoying the moment. "It's been a long time since you've been caught in the act, Joe. Looks like you've perfected the craft along the way."

Joe rolled his eyes at the comment. "I didn't steal that catbird painting or anything else around here. You're on the wrong track."

"I know that, Joe," Abby assured him, anxious to clear up the misunderstanding. "I had no idea that Mr. Briley intended to accuse you."

"Look, folks," Briley said. "You two are friends, so this doesn't have to get messy. If Joe just returns the items—"

"I didn't take them," Joe said between clenched teeth. "Just because I did something stupid as a teenager doesn't make me a career criminal."

"You have a record," Briley said. "That's indisputable."

"I stole a cheap bracelet," Joe exclaimed, "because I was young and stupid and wanted to impress some silly girl who lived next door. Believe me, I learned my lesson when she saw me hauled away in handcuffs. I never did anything like that again."

"How old were you?" Abby asked softly.

Joe turned toward the window, unable to face her. "Eighteen and poor as a church mouse. That twenty-dollar bracelet cost me my job and my self-respect. I thought I had put it all behind me . . . until today."

Abby felt sick inside. Why did Briley have to drag up that painful memory from the past? It had happened over fifty years ago. Joe Blackstock was one of the kindest, most honest men she knew.

"I'm so sorry," Abby told him, placing a hand on his arm. "I had no idea."

"Neither does Margaret," Joe said softly. "I'd appreciate if you didn't say anything to her about it."

"Of course not," Abby promised him.

Briley moved toward the door. "So you're sticking to your story, Joe?"

Joe turned to face him. "It's not a story, it's the truth. I was at dinner with everyone when Abby's painting was stolen and I was out taking a walk when that teapot disappeared. I dare you to prove otherwise."

"Okay, then," Briley headed toward the door. "Thanks for your help."

Abby followed him out the door. "How could you do that to him?"

"Sometimes you have to push a few buttons to get somebody to crack. Blackstock didn't crack, so I think we can cross him off the list."

"You mean you brought up his past and embarrassed him for nothing?"

"It wasn't for nothing." Briley pushed the button on the elevator. "We eliminated one of the possible suspects, didn't we?"

Abby knew he'd accomplished much more than that. He'd hurt one of her good friends, a man she liked and respected. After the short time she'd spent in Bill Briley's company, Abby didn't want to deal with him and his tactics anymore.

CHAPTER ✤ SIXTEEN

Tʜᴀᴛ ᴇᴠᴇɴɪɴɢ, ᴀʙʙʏ emerged from the bathroom with the floral aroma of her hairspray still lingering in the air. She saw her sister reclined on her bed with a book open in her lap.

"You'd better start getting ready for the reception," Abby told her. "It starts in less than an hour."

Mary closed the book. "I'm not going."

Abby's heart sank. Her sister had hardly been out of the hotel room since retrieving Finnegan from the animal control facility yesterday. "You have to go. Everyone will be there and I know we'll have fun."

"I'm tired," Mary explained, "and I'm expecting a call from Henry later. I don't want to miss it."

Abby wanted to say more, but she restrained herself as she finished dressing. She didn't want to push Mary into doing something that made her uncomfortable. Yet, she didn't want to leave her all alone in the room tonight, either.

"Maybe I should stay in too." Abby adjusted the watchband on her wrist. "We could play cards or watch a movie."

"Absolutely not," Mary insisted. "You have another date with Marcus and I'm not about to let you disappoint him." She pointed to her jewelry case. "Why don't you wear my silver bracelet? It would look perfect with your dress."

Abby walked over to take the bracelet out of the case. "Are you sure you won't come? Finnegan would probably enjoy the exercise."

"Amanda Pederson volunteered to take him for a long walk earlier today," Mary replied, "so he's had plenty of exercise. Besides, I've already taken off my makeup and I don't feel like getting dressed and doing my hair. I just want to relax."

Abby wished she could believe her. She sensed that Mary's reluctance to go to the party had more to do with running into Susan Pederson again or someone just like her. She hated the fact that such attitudes made Mary a virtual prisoner in her own hotel room.

"Please don't worry about me," Mary told her sister. "If I change my mind, I know where to find you."

"I hope you do change your mind," Abby said, as her sister picked up her book and began reading once more.

There was nothing more she could say, not to Mary anyway. She closed her eyes and whispered a prayer for her sister.

A HALF AN HOUR LATER, Marcus escorted Abby into the grand ballroom of the hotel for the *Antique Adventures* reception. The show had gone all out to make their guests feel special.

Decorative lights twinkled like stars on the ceiling above them and each of the round tables was covered with a white linen tablecloth and set with the finest china, silver and crystal.

A dessert buffet table spanned the length of one wall and

contained a wide variety of delicacies. There were chocolate fountains and even an ice sculpture with the show's emblem as the main centerpiece.

Abby looked for Joe among the crowd of people, but she didn't see him. She still felt badly about Briley's treatment of him and wanted another chance to apologize for it. What hurt her the most was Joe's apparent belief that she was on Briley's side rather than his.

The hotel detective seemed to have a talent for digging up dirt on people. She just wished he had a talent for investigation. So far, she wasn't impressed. Briley seemed more suited to working for a tabloid newspaper than hotel security. Perhaps that was one of the reasons he had retired from the police department early.

Marcus stood beside her looking more handsome than ever in his black tuxedo. He was one of the few men who had dressed formally for the reception, but he didn't look out of place.

"Shall we look for your friends?" Marcus asked her. "Or find a table just for the two of us?"

Abby had been so distracted by the case that she'd barely said two words to Marcus. "I don't see anyone here yet that I know, so why don't we just find a table?"

He smiled. "Perfect."

They walked to a far corner table and he pulled a chair out for her.

"Did I mention how lovely you look tonight?" Marcus asked her as he seated himself beside her.

Abby was growing so used to his compliments that she didn't even blush anymore. Her sister had picked out the white silk blouse with the black pearl buttons and matching black slacks. Casual, but elegant, it seemed to fit the occasion perfectly.

"Thank you," Abby said. "You look very handsome yourself."

"How about a glass of punch?" Marcus offered.

Before she could reply, a woman approached their table. "Marcus Wolfe, is that you?"

The woman had just the slightest hint of a southern accent and reminded Abby of a fashion model. Tall, lithe and blonde, the red dress the woman wore hugged her slender figure.

He rose to his feet. "Hello, Valerie. How are you this evening?"

Abby ventured a guess that this was the fellow antiques dealer he'd spoken to her about during their lunch date. When she'd told him she didn't feel comfortable posing as a buyer, he'd accepted her answer with his usual grace and charm.

"I'm wonderful," Valerie replied, reaching out to shake his hand. Only she didn't let go of it. "And I can see you are the same. I believe you grow more handsome every year."

Marcus turned to Abby. "I'd like to introduce you to a colleague of mine. This is Valerie Lendl. Valerie, this is Dr. Abby Stanton."

"A pleasure," Valerie said with a slight nod of her head. "Are you in the business?"

"Oh no." Abby smiled. "I'm an ornithologist and the Associate Curator of the Sparrow Island Nature Conservatory."

"Ah." Valerie's blue eyes sparkled. "The San Juan Islands are so beautiful and peaceful. I spent a wonderful vacation there a few years ago."

"Marcus told me you're an antiques dealer," Abby observed. "Did you bring something to the show or are you here to buy?"

Valerie laughed. "I'm what you call an *Antique Adventures*

groupie, just like Marcus. We follow the show from city to city, hoping to pick up a few treasures along the way."

Abby hadn't realized that this wasn't Marcus's first show. She wondered why he hadn't mentioned it before. "That sounds interesting."

"Oh, it is," Valerie affirmed. "We're introduced to so many fascinating people. Like you, Dr. Stanton. I've never met an ornithologist before. You must tell me all about it."

"I'll leave you two to get acquainted while I get us some punch." Marcus winked at Abby and headed for the buffet table.

Valerie watched him leave, then scooted her chair closer to Abby. "Now that it's just us girls, tell me all about you and Marcus."

"There's not much to tell," she replied honestly. "We met on the *Victoria Clipper* on Monday and discovered that we enjoy each other's company."

"I'm not surprised." Valerie smiled. "Marcus likes to collect interesting women."

"I'm not sure what you mean."

"Nothing insulting, I assure you." She tucked her hair behind one ear. "Marcus is a darling, he truly is. A bit of a wolf, like his name implies, but always the perfect gentleman."

Abby wondered if this would be a good time to do a little investigative work. Anything to get Valerie off the subject of her friendship with Marcus.

"How long have you been following the show?"

Valerie pursed her lips. "*Hmmm*, almost three years now. It's something of an addiction for me."

"So you know a lot of the cast and crew, like Dr. Houston and Sylvia Pierce?"

"Very well." Valerie leaned in. "Although word has it that Dr. Houston won't be on the road much longer. He's missed the mark on a few of his appraisals. All within the margin of error, but enough for the suits upstairs to take notice."

Abby had heard this rumor before and wondered if it could be connected to the odd thefts occurring at the shows. She decided to ask Valerie about them.

"Thefts?" Valerie echoed when she brought up the subject. "Oh, you mean the prankster who steals the antiques, then gives them back right before the show? If you ask me, it's probably some lowly crew member who likes to see his bosses panic and create a little drama to break the monotony."

"Do you have anyone particular in mind who'd do that sort of thing?"

"Not at all." Valerie adjusted the sapphire necklace around her throat. "I guess I just always assumed it was someone near the bottom of the proverbial food chain. One of the errand boys or a guy on the construction crew or something."

"How about somebody higher up?"

She shrugged. "I wish I could unveil the thief for you and become the heroine of the hour, but I truly have no idea who the culprit might be."

"Has anyone ever considered setting a trap for him?" Abby ventured.

"A trap?" Valerie stared at her, then a slow smile spread across her face. "You *are* an interesting woman, Dr. Stanton. I can see why Marcus is attracted to you. He's no doubt fascinated by the combination of your intellect and tenacious curiosity."

Abby decided to take that as a compliment. And she was still waiting for Valerie to answer her question.

"I'm afraid no one has been quite that creative in trying to find a solution to the problem." Valerie rose from her chair. "I can tell you that some of the crew do take bets, though, on which antique will be stolen when they go through the evaluation process."

Abby watched her flick her long blonde hair over her shoulder.

"So far," Valerie continued, "the majority of the stolen items are from Dr. Houston's category if that means anything. Perhaps he's trying to draw attention away from his appraisal errors or make his superiors think about something else besides trying to force him to retire."

Abby knew it might mean a lot or nothing at all. But if Valerie was right about Dr. Houston, that did give him a motive.

"Please say good-bye to Marcus for me." Valerie slung her tiny black sequin purse over her shoulder. "And tell him I look forward to seeing him in Toronto next week. Let's just hope they don't have one of their early snowstorms again."

Abby watched her walk away, the swing of her hips causing more than one man in the room to look in her direction.

"I'm sorry it took me so long," Marcus said, returning with two glasses of punch. Then he gave her a sheepish smile. "All right, I'll confess I was waiting until Valerie left. That woman never stops talking."

Abby didn't mind. Valerie's chattiness had helped her learn more about the behind-the-scenes action of *Antique Adventures* and perhaps moved her one step closer to finding out who stole her catbird.

Valerie's conversation had also stirred an uneasiness inside of Abby that made her look at Marcus in a different light. The woman had called him a wolf, though Abby usually gave little credence to such talk, especially from a stranger.

Yet, she wondered why Marcus hadn't told her that he followed the *Antique Adventures* show from town to town. Was he a groupie, too, like Valerie?

And what other secrets was he keeping from her?

She could no longer overlook Marcus as a suspect in the theft, no matter how charming she found him. He'd made her an inflated offer for her gray catbird picture without knowing its value. Unless he knew more about the painting than he'd let on.

"You haven't touched your punch," Marcus observed. "Is anything wrong?"

Before she could reply, Abby saw a few of her Sparrow Island friends heading straight for their table. Marcus stood up to greet them, shaking hands with Hugo, Naomi and Lindsey.

Hugo sat beside Abby. "I've seen that look on your face before," he said quietly. "Care to share your thoughts?"

She wanted nothing more than to confide in Hugo, but now wasn't the time or the place. Besides, she wasn't ready to voice her suspicion aloud, not until she had more proof other than the uneasy feeling inside of her.

The hurt and bewilderment she'd seen on Joe's face at being falsely accused was still too fresh in her mind to allow it to happen again. Unlike Bill Briley, she intended to have all the facts to prove her case before she pointed the finger at anybody.

Abby forced a smile. "I'm just taking it all in. This is such a new experience for me. The week's going by much too quickly."

Hugo nodded. "I hope we have another chance to tour that museum before we leave."

"So do I," Abby replied, realizing they hadn't spent much time together since their arrival. It occurred to her that she saw more of Hugo while they were working at the conservatory than she had while staying at the same hotel.

Naomi looked around the ballroom. "They really put on quite a party, don't they?"

"It's the least they can do," Marcus replied, "since they're not paying for any of you to appear on their television show. Believe me, they're saving money in the long run."

Abby took a sip of her cranberry punch, but found it too sweet for her taste. She put the cup back down, then began to wonder why Joe wasn't there yet. She hoped he wasn't holed up in his room, too embarrassed to join the group after Briley's attempt to paint him as the thief.

"Where's Joe?" Hugo asked, noting his absence as well. "Has anyone seen him?"

"I stopped by his room," Naomi said, "but there was no answer when I knocked. I assumed he was here."

Abby looked down at the table, knowing she couldn't tell any of them what happened without revealing Joe's secret.

"Mary's not here, either." Hugo looked at Abby. "Is she ill?"

"No, just tired," Abby replied. "She and Finnegan decided to stay in for the evening."

Frustration gripped her as she looked around the table, too aware of the empty places there. She'd continue to pray for Mary and add Joe to her prayers as well. She'd also intensify her search for the real culprit before Briley did any more damage.

"There's Thelma," Lindsey cried, raising her hand to wave her down. "Looks like Betty's with her too."

Abby looked up, curious to see the long-lost sister. Betty was the spitting image of Thelma, with the same thin build and puffs of hair atop her head. Seeing them together, Abby couldn't help but smile.

ABBY STOOD ON THE BALCONY outside the ballroom, gazing up at the sky. It was cooler out there and a welcome relief from the loud music that the band had started playing an hour ago.

"There you are," Hugo said, coming up behind her. "I wondered where you'd gone."

"I'd forgotten how difficult it was to see the stars in the city," she said, still looking up. "They always seem so bright and close on Sparrow Island."

Hugo joined her at the rail, his face tilted toward the sky. "You sound homesick."

"I guess I am a little," she admitted, "which is rather silly since I lived away from home for over three decades."

"Not silly to me," he said softly. Hugo turned to face her. "I'm sorry we haven't been able to spend more time together on this trip, Abby. I was looking forward to associating outside of work for a change."

His words touched her. "Me too. I've been so caught up in trying to find my catbird painting and helping Mary with Finnegan and—"

"Marcus," he interjected, turning to face the night sky once more. "I noticed the two of you seem to be spending a lot of time together."

"Not really," Abby countered. "We had lunch yesterday and he escorted me to the reception this evening. He's a very interesting man."

Hugo nodded. "I assume he must be to have captured your attention."

Abby stared at him. Hugo almost sounded a bit jealous. Then again, if he'd been spending time with another woman during their trip, she might be feeling a little left out too.

"Are you free for breakfast tomorrow?" she asked him. "I'd

love to hear your impression of the *Antique Adventures* show so far."

He smiled. "I am free. Around eight o'clock or would you prefer to meet earlier?"

"Eight sounds perfect to me." Abby's heart lightened. She might have doubts about Marcus, but Hugo was a stalwart friend in her life. He'd never let her down.

"If the weather's nice," Abby ventured, "maybe we can eat in the hotel courtyard. I'd like a chance to just people-watch for a while."

"One of my favorite activities," Hugo agreed. "I've been doing a little of that myself today and came across something rather interesting."

"Oh?"

He gave a small shrug. "I'm not sure it's anything significant, but I saw your appraiser, Dr. Houston, arguing with one of the hotel maids last night."

That got Abby's attention. "Where did this happen?"

"Near the service elevators. I was taking one of my late-night strolls and came across them while they were in the middle of a heated conversation."

"Can you describe the maid?

"Average height. Dark hair pulled back into a ponytail."

"That fits the description Mr. Okafor gave me, except her hair was down instead of up. Of course, his description also fits over half the maids in this hotel. That's the problem."

"I wish I could tell you more," Hugo continued. "I didn't hear any of their conversation. They stopped talking as soon as they saw me."

Dr. Houston was quickly gaining ground as the lead suspect.

An experienced appraiser, he knew the value of her catbird painting. Perhaps he'd bribed this maid to steal it for him and now she was causing him trouble. Maybe even black-mailing him.

"So how's your investigation coming along?" Hugo asked her.

Abby sighed. "I feel like it's moving at a snail's pace. Especially since I only have a couple of days left to solve it before we have to go home." Then she squared her shoulders. "But as long as I keep moving forward, I'm bound to come across something valuable."

He chuckled. "Always the optimist. That's one of the things I like best about you, Abby."

His kind words warmed her heart and stole her tongue.

"So have you ruled anyone out yet?"

She thought about his question. "I don't consider any of my Sparrow Island friends as suspects, although I can't seem to convince Mr. Briley of that."

"He does seem somewhat brash."

That was putting it mildly. Her hand tightened on the balcony rail when she thought of the way Briley had treated Joe.

Abby sighed. "That leaves someone on the crew of the show as the most likely suspect. Since Jeffrey, Chloe, Ned and Hans were all with me when Betty's teapot was stolen, they're in the clear."

Then she told him about the past thefts at *Antique Adventures* and how the stolen items had a way of turning up again right before taping was due to begin.

Hugo looked intrigued. "So there's a chance you might get your catbird painting back even if you don't catch the thief?"

"Jeffrey and his friends seemed convinced of it. They look at the thefts as more of a prank than a crime, though I don't share their opinion."

"Neither do I," Hugo said. "Not when people are hurt in the process."

"I need to keep an open mind about this investigation," Abby said, more to remind herself than anything else. "It could be anyone."

Hugo moved a step closer to her. "I wish I could be of more help to you."

She looked up at him. "Just being able to talk to you about it helps more than you'll ever know."

He smiled. "That's what friends are for."

Marcus stepped onto the balcony. "I hope I'm not interrupting."

Abby cleared her throat. "Not at all. Hugo and I were just enjoying the night air."

"Not quite the same as the San Juan Islands, is it?" Marcus said, moving next to Abby.

Hugo glanced at Marcus, then out at the skyline. "It's a different world, although I do enjoy spending time in the big city. And there's nothing like a skyline lit up at night."

"True," Marcus agreed, then turned to Abby. "They just brought in another dessert cart and it looks delicious. Would you like to join me?"

He held out his arm and Abby hesitated a moment, looking between the two men. Then she said, "Of course. Hugo, are you coming?"

"I think I'll enjoy the night air for a bit longer," he replied. "You two go ahead."

They left the balcony and walked back into the ballroom. Abby scanned the room for Betty, still wanting to talk to her, but she saw no sign of either her or Thelma.

"You look tired," Marcus observed. "Perhaps we should skip dessert and call it a night."

"Would you mind?" Abby asked, feeling as if she'd like nothing better than a good night's sleep. She was also anxious to check on her absent sister.

"Not at all." He led her to the ballroom doors, then turned and took both of her hands in his own. She inhaled the spicy scent of his cologne and felt the warmth of his hands around her fingers.

"Thank you for a lovely evening, Marcus. Will I see you tomorrow?"

He leaned over to gently kiss her cheek. "You can count on it."

CHAPTER 🌣 SEVENTEEN

I'VE MADE A DECISION," Mary announced Thursday morning.

Abby stood in front of the full-length mirror, putting the finishing touches on her hair. She was due to meet Hugo for breakfast in fifteen minutes and had a full day ahead of her. Her sister had been fast asleep when she'd returned to the room the night before, so she hadn't had a chance to talk to her.

"Finnegan and I are not going to stay cooped up in this hotel room anymore," Mary continued, a defiant tone in her voice. "We're here on vacation and it's about time we start enjoying ourselves."

The dog's head popped up at the sound of his name. He padded over to Mary and stood beside her wheelchair, ready for action.

Abby breathed a sigh of relief. She'd feared that Mary was going to announce that she was headed back to Sparrow Island. "I'm so glad to hear it."

Mary rolled her wheelchair closer to her sister. "So what's on your agenda this morning?"

"Well, I'm meeting Hugo for breakfast, then I need to talk to Betty about the theft of her teapot, show up for the locket taping at ten o'clock, then meet Jeffrey for lunch at noon."

"My," Mary exclaimed, "you do have a full schedule. I think you're busier on your vacation than you are working at the conservatory."

Abby laughed. "I think you may be right. My days certainly seem more hectic. Although . . ."

"What?" Mary prodded.

"I'm not sure if I should appear on *Antique Adventures* with Grandma Lora's locket. Maybe you were right before. Some things might be better left in the past."

"What brought this on?" Mary inquired. "I think Mom would be thrilled to hear her mother's story on television. Grandma Lora had such faith and courage."

Abby hadn't told her sister what she'd found out about the locket, hating to tarnish their beloved grandmother's memory. But she wasn't going to lie to her either.

"After my meeting with the jewelry appraiser," Abby began, "I did some research on Nigel Black, the goldsmith she told me had made the locket."

Mary arched a brow. "And?"

"And this particular locket was one of a kind," Abby continued, "custom made for an important client of Nigel Black. The locket apparently disappeared from his store during the same month Grandma Lora boarded the orphan train leaving New York City."

"Disappeared?" Mary echoed. "Are you saying that Grandma Lora stole the locket?"

Abby shrugged. "It would explain why she never wanted to talk about her past or tell us where the locket came from."

"It's not possible," Mary insisted. "Grandma Lora was not a thief."

"We don't know what she had to do to survive," Abby reminded her sister. "She was only eleven years old. Her mother was ill. She was facing an uncertain future with no money and no one to take care of her until she was adopted by a new family."

Mary looked ashen. "You're right. We have no idea what she went through or how frightened she must have been to leave her home forever."

Abby nodded. "The only way they could communicate was through letters, and Grandma Lora didn't even know where she was going. And it's not like her mother had a permanent residence. From what little she did reveal about her past, it sounded as if they were always on the move."

"Even homeless at times," Mary added.

"So if I go to the taping," Abby said, "the story about the stolen locket is very likely to come out. After all, it only took me a few minutes on the computer to find it. Do we really want to sully Grandma Lora's memory that way?"

"I see what you mean," Mary said, realizing the implications.

Abby adjusted the bracelet on her wrist. "That's why I'm not sure what to do. I've even prayed about it."

They fell into silence, each struggling with the dilemma before them. Finnegan looked between the two of them, his tail wagging slowly.

"Mom really wanted me to have the locket appraised," Abby said at last. "It means so much to her because it meant so much to her mother."

"I know," Mary said softly.

Abby reached for her purse and removed the locket. She held it by the fine gold chain, the small oval slowly swinging from side to side. Inside the locket was a tiny lock of faded red hair, the only memento young Lora had of her mother when she boarded the orphan train.

A mother she'd never seen again.

"I think you should go on the show." Mary rolled her wheelchair closer to her sister. "For good or for bad, that locket is part of her history, of *our* family history. We can't be afraid of it."

Abby considered her words. "Rev. Hale always tells us not to hide from the truth." She took a deep breath. "All right, I'll do it. I'll go to the taping."

Mary smiled. "I think that's the right decision. It won't air for a few weeks, so we can prepare Mom ahead of time for what to expect."

Abby reached for her jacket. "I'd better get moving if I want to make it to breakfast in time. I'm not sure how I'm going to fit everything in today."

"Why don't you let me help?" Mary offered. "I can talk to Betty and hear her story, then we can meet back here in time to go to the locket taping together."

"Would you?" Abby replied, pleased her sister wanted to take an active role in helping her solve this mystery. "That would be wonderful."

"I'll pop over to her room first thing," Mary said, then she smiled at her sister. "You look very nice."

Abby glanced down at her camel jacket and brown slacks. "Thank you. I'm glad you suggested I bring it along."

"Here," Mary said, moving toward her suitcases. "Why don't you wear my gold hoop earrings? They're perfect for the outfit."

Abby took the earrings from her and put them on. Then she studied herself in the mirror, amazed once again at her sister's good fashion sense. "You're right. They're perfect."

"You'd better scoot." Mary told her. "You don't want to keep Hugo waiting."

Abby grabbed her purse off the bed. "I'm anxious to hear what Betty has to say."

"I'll take good notes," Mary promised, escorting her sister to the door.

After Abby left the hotel room, Mary turned to Finnegan. "Time for us to go play detective. Are you ready, Watson?"

The dog stood very still as Mary placed his service cape and harness on him. Then she cupped his sweet face in her hands. "I'm sorry I've made you stay in this room for so long. We're going out in public now, so it's the perfect time to show everyone what a wonderful dog you are."

Finnegan blinked at her, his tail wagging in anticipation.

Mary took a deep breath, hoping they didn't encounter any more problems. The few times she'd taken Finnegan outside the hotel to exercise, they'd received tentative glances from some of the hotel staff. No doubt the news of Finnegan nipping one of the employees had already spread and probably been embellished along the way.

Mary wanted Finnegan to redeem himself and knew that he would if she just gave him a chance.

Fifteen minutes later, they were knocking at Betty's door.

They'd made the trek from the third floor to the fifth without incident.

"So far, so good," Mary murmured.

Finnegan stood at attention beside her wheelchair, ready for her next command.

The door opened and Betty smiled when she saw them on the other side. "Hello."

"Hello, Betty. I'm Mary Reynolds. Abby Stanton's sister. I hope you don't mind a couple of early morning visitors."

"Not at all," Betty said, opening the door wider to let them in. "I've been up for hours. I guess I'm still on Florida time."

"How are you enjoying Seattle?"

Betty smiled. "Very much. This is my first trip to the West Coast. Hard to believe since Thelma's lived here for so many years."

"You have a lovely view," Mary said, moving her wheelchair toward the window. "I can even see the Space Needle from here."

"The view is even better in this room than it was in my first one." Betty stood beside Mary. "The hotel gave me a smoking room when I first arrived. I knew as soon as I walked in the door that I couldn't stay there. I didn't even unpack. I've got terrible allergies."

"So you switched rooms?"

Betty nodded. "Poor Thelma was so confused when she tried to call me about meeting for lunch. I'd forgotten she still had my original room number."

Mary gave Finnegan the signal to relax and he sat down next to her.

"He's such a lovely dog," Betty observed. "Can I get something for him? Some water, perhaps?"

"He's fine," Mary told her. She'd fed Finnegan and seen him lap up a bowl of water before they'd left.

"How about you?" Betty asked. "I have some fresh coffee ready."

"That sounds wonderful."

Mary watched her while she poured the coffee, astonished by the close resemblance between Betty and her sister. "If I didn't know better, I'd say you and Thelma could be twins."

Betty laughed. "We used to hear that all the time. Of course, part of the reason for that was because our mother always liked to dress us in identical outfits."

"Are you close in age?"

"Less than a year apart," Betty responded. "I was born one week before Thelma's first birthday, so we were the same age for one week every year. Boy, Thelma used to really hate that."

Mary smiled. "I can imagine."

Betty handed her a cup of steaming coffee. "So what brings you here this morning?"

Mary leaned back in her wheelchair. "Abby wanted me to ask you about the day your teapot was stolen."

A shadow passed over Betty's face. "Oh."

Mary felt badly for broaching the unpleasant subject when they were having such a nice conversation. Still, it had to be done.

"Abby's catbird painting is still missing," Mary reminded her, "and she's trying to determine who the culprit might be. She thought if we compared notes between the theft in our room and the one in yours, we might come up with some possible clues to lead us in the right direction."

Betty sighed. "I'm not sure what I can tell you, Mary. When my sister and I returned from lunch, the teapot was gone."

"Thelma mentioned that the room was a mess."

Betty nodded. "Yes, everything was strewn about. I hadn't even finished unpacking yet. I can only imagine that the thief was searching for something valuable to steal."

"Was anything else taken?"

Betty shook her head. "Just the teapot. I still can't believe it's gone."

Mary took a sip of her coffee, then thought of another question. "Was your hotel room door open when you returned from lunch or locked?"

"It was still locked. I had to use my key card to get inside."

"And you didn't see anyone when you left to go meet Thelma at the restaurant?"

"No . . ." Betty began, then looked up at her. "Well, there was a maid in the hallway, but that's hardly unusual."

It might not be unusual, but if it was the same maid Mr. Okafor had seen then it might be more than a coincidence.

"Can you describe her?" Mary asked.

Betty grimaced. "To tell you the truth, I really wasn't paying much attention. I was so anxious about seeing Thelma again after all these years that I just walked right past her."

"Do you remember anything about her?" Mary persisted. "Anything at all."

Betty thought for a long moment. "I think she had dark hair. Other than that, nothing stands out in my mind. I'm sorry."

Mary swallowed a sigh. It wasn't much, but it was better than nothing. "That's all right. Any little bit of information helps."

"There's really no hope though, is there?" Betty said.

"I mean that the teapot or your sister's catbird painting will ever be recovered. The thief is probably long gone by now."

"We're not ready to give up yet," Mary assured her. "Abby thinks the thief may be connected to the show in some capacity since there have been other thefts at other *Antique Adventures* venues. In the past, many of those stolen items have been returned."

"But not all of them?"

"No," Mary said, sorry to disappoint her. "Not all of them."

Betty shook her head in dismay. "You'd think the show would hire a guard or something to protect all the antiques."

"It's a little surprising that they're not more concerned about it." Mary took another sip of her coffee. "Of course, they have hundreds of people coming through with their treasures in a matter of days. I suppose they can't take responsibility for all of them."

"No," Betty agreed, "that would be an impossible task."

"Let's just hope that the painting and your teapot are returned."

Betty didn't look optimistic. "I'd hate to get my hopes up only to be disappointed again."

"I understand." Mary finished her coffee, then set the empty cup on the table beside her. "Is there anything else you can tell me about the theft?"

"Like what?"

Mary shrugged. "Anything unusual that happened either before or after your lunch with Thelma?"

Betty pursed her lips. "*Hmm.* Let me think about it."

Mary waited, hoping something would come to her.

"I wish there was," Betty said at last. "But I can't think of a thing. I'm so sorry."

"That's all right," Mary assured her, signaling Finnegan that it was time to go.

"I feel like I've let you down," Betty said, walking her to the door. "And Thelma, of course. I should have hidden the teapot as soon as I got to my room. Or even put it in the hotel safe."

"I'm sure Thelma doesn't blame you."

"I'm not so sure," Betty said quietly. "She was devastated when we got back to my room and found the teapot missing. I'll never forget the look on her face." A sob caught in Betty's throat, but she swallowed it back. "I'm sorry. It's just so difficult."

"I know." Mary reached out to pat her arm. "At least you have each other to help you through it."

Betty gave a small nod, then opened the door for her. "Thank you so much for stopping by."

"Thank you for the coffee," Mary replied, carefully easing her wheelchair between the tight fit of the door frame. When she was out in the hallway, she turned around to face Betty. "And don't worry, there's still a chance that you might get your teapot back."

Betty gave her a tight smile. "That would be wonderful."

Mary rolled down the hallway, feeling as if she'd accomplished something. She couldn't wait to meet with Abby later and tell her Betty's story.

When she reached the elevator, Mary gave Finnegan the command to press the down button. He did so, and a few moments later the doors slid open.

That's when Mary saw Susan Pederson standing alone inside the elevator.

CHAPTER ❦ EIGHTEEN

ABBY SPENT A LEISURELY breakfast with Hugo. They chatted about future plans for the conservatory and both lost track of the time. That happened so often with her boss. Their passion for their work often kept them talking together for hours.

After they left the restaurant, Abby checked her cell phone messages and found one from Bill Briley.

"Hey, I think I've got a live one for you, maybe two. Why don't you come to my office as soon as you get this message."

"Oh no," Abby muttered, returning her cell phone to her bag.

"Is something wrong?" Hugo asked.

"It seems Mr. Briley is on duty again."

Abby was doubly grateful that Mary had offered to interview Thelma's sister, since she'd barely have time to see Briley before going to the taping. She was glad she'd waited until after breakfast to check her messages because it would have spoiled her appetite.

"I think you should fire him from the case," Hugo suggested, a twinkle in his blue eyes. "In my humble opinion, you have much better investigative skills and much nicer manners."

If only it were that easy, she thought. By the time she reached Briley's office she saw that he'd already started without her.

Lindsey Buckminster and Naomi Yardley sat in the chairs opposite his desk, both looking more than a little apprehensive.

"What's going on here?" Abby asked Briley.

He sat on the corner of his desk, a notepad in one hand and a pencil in the other. "I just asked your friends to come in and have another little powwow with me about the recent thefts."

"Thefts have been occurring at every venue where the show tapes," Abby reminded him. "So I think that eliminates them as suspects. Besides, I told you they were both at dinner with me when the painting was stolen."

"So you did." Briley tapped his pencil on the desk. "A convenient alibi. However, I decided to do a little more digging and discovered a few more interesting facts about your neighbors."

Abby closed her eyes, praying for patience. She'd tried to give Briley the benefit of the doubt, but he seemed to enjoy alienating her friends.

"I don't care what you dug up," Abby said. "We both know that no one from Sparrow Island could possibly be the thief."

"You have to admit that it seems like more than a coincidence that the two thefts were connected to your group. There are hundreds of people here for the *Antique Adventures* show."

Abby realized it did look suspicious and in any other circumstance she might agree with him, but every instinct told her that Briley was wrong.

"I believe it's simply a process of elimination, Dr. Stanton. I wouldn't expect a layman to understand. Or a laywoman, as the case may be." He pulled a handkerchief out of his back pocket and loudly blew his nose. "I've found something that may implicate your two friends here. Or at least give them a motive."

"What?" Naomi asked, looking worried. "Is it something bad?"

He zeroed in on her. "Why don't you tell me, Ms. Yardley? Is there anything you'd like to confess right now?"

"Our personal lives are none of your business," Lindsey sputtered. "I can't believe you called us down here to accuse us—"

"I haven't accused you of anything yet," Briley interjected. His casual manner belied the cunning gleam in his eyes.

"Then why did you insist we meet you here this morning?" Lindsey asked. "I already had plans to go shopping."

He lifted a brow in her direction. "I'm not sure that's wise, given your circumstances."

Lindsey's cheeks grew pink, then she looked down at the floor.

Briley consulted his notepad. "This won't take long, ladies. I just wanted to clarify a few things for the investigation." He pointed to a folding chair in the corner. "Go ahead and have a seat, Dr. Stanton. You might as well be comfortable."

Abby carried the folding chair over to Lindsey and Naomi, setting it up between them. She wanted Briley to have no doubt as to whose side she was on.

"Let's start with Ms. Buckminster," Briley began, slipping on his bifocals as he turned to Lindsey. "I believe you own a horse ranch?"

"Yes, Lindsey replied. "Summit Stables. Why?"

"Raising horses is quite an expensive proposition, isn't it?"

Lindsey tipped up her chin. "I do all right."

"Do you?" Briley consulted his notes. "Then why was your credit card turned down when you tried to check into the hotel on Monday?"

Lindsey's cheeks turned a bright pink. "I can explain."

"It seems obvious to me," Briley told her. "Your business is in serious financial difficulty. That certainly gives you a motive for theft, doesn't it?"

Abby could see the mortification in Lindsey's eyes as painful details of her personal life were being dragged out in front of them.

Lindsey turned to Abby and Naomi, her face taut. "One of my colts broke his leg. Instead of having him put down, I asked my vet to treat him. It was very expensive and as the costs mounted I started applying them to the credit card until it reached the limit. I've worked out a payment plan with the vet and it's all resolved now. I am not the thief."

"Of course you're not," Abby assured her, then stared down Briley. "Lindsey and I went to high school together. She's one of the most honest people I know."

Briley gave a small shrug, then turned his attention to Naomi. "Then perhaps Ms. Yardley had more motivation to steal. More *personal* motivation."

Naomi stiffened. "I don't know what you mean."

"Don't you?" He flipped a page on a notepad. "According to my information, your elderly mother recently moved into an assisted living home in Phoenix. Those places can be quite expensive, and I bet she depends on her only daughter to help her out financially."

"I do what I can," Naomi countered. "That doesn't include stealing."

"Then where do you get the items that you sell on eBay?" Briley asked. "I took a look at your account and noticed a large selection of books available for sale. Have you been pilfering from your library?"

Naomi's nostrils flared. "We get book donations that we can't always use and the library board has given me permission to sell them on my personal eBay account to raise money for the library. I keep records of all the transactions and turn them over to the board secretary every month."

Briley didn't look convinced. "Perhaps you decided to expand your eBay sales to include a bird painting and a teapot."

"Naomi wouldn't sell something on eBay that could so easily be traced back to her," said Abby.

Naomi turned to face Abby. "Does that mean you think I might have stolen them too?"

"Of course not," Abby protested, realizing too late how it must have sounded to Naomi. "I know that you're innocent. You're *both* innocent."

"Innocent people are often provoked into doing things they never dreamed of doing when pushed into a corner," Briley opined. "I've seen it countless times. Money is the most common motivation."

He tossed his notepad onto his desk. "Motivation that both Ms. Buckminster and Ms. Yardley seem to have in spades."

Lindsey jumped to her feet. "I won't sit here and let you accuse me of stealing." Then she turned to Abby. "I can't believe you're making us endure this insulting interrogation over a ten-dollar picture!"

Before Abby could reply, Lindsey was out the door with Naomi right on her heels.

"Looks like I pushed a few buttons," Briley said, a smile playing on his mouth. "Maybe if I push a few more something will finally shift loose and we'll be able to solve this case."

Abby stared at him, wondering if this style really worked for him. "I think we should shift our focus from my friends from Sparrow Island to the personnel of *Antique Adventures*."

"Hey, I'm open to suggestions. If you have something, bring it to me and we'll go from there." He reached for a half-eaten donut on his desk. "In the meantime, I'll keep digging and see what I can find out."

Abby left his office more frustrated than ever. She was tempted to go straight to Mr. Eames and make him take the annoying detective off the case.

Maybe Lindsey was right and she was making too much trouble over a ten-dollar picture. But Betty's English teapot was missing, too, and that had a sizable, determined value.

She thought about Jeffrey's contention that the painting and the teapot might be returned before the week was over. If that happened, Joe and Lindsey and Naomi would have all suffered through Mr. Briley's intrusive interviews for nothing.

She paused to take a deep breath and consider all her options. It was possible she'd been trying to shoulder too much of this burden on her own—an easy thing to do when she lost track of the priorities in her life.

She didn't need to turn to Briley for help, but to God.

Abby changed direction and headed for the hotel courtyard.

She walked over to the flower garden and sat down on a stone bench. The sun had warmed it and Abby began to relax as she watched the fall aster blossoms swing gently in the breeze.

"Heavenly Father," she prayed softly, "please give me guidance as I seek the right path. Let me do Your will and not my own. Show me the way, Lord. Amen."

Abby sat on the bench awhile longer, the peaceful garden and her heartfelt prayer helping her to refocus. She wanted to find a way to heal the strife among her friends and neighbors.

"WE CAN WAIT for the next elevator," Mary told Susan Pederson, her adrenaline pumping in her veins. More than anything, she wanted to avoid another ugly confrontation. "You go ahead."

"No, that's all right," Susan replied, her face taut as she stared at Finnegan. "There's room in here for both of you."

Mary hesitated, not thrilled at the idea of being trapped in an elevator with this woman. But she had decided just this morning not to live in fear anymore. She had as much right to ride the elevator as any other guest of the Bristol Hotel.

She signaled for Finnegan to move forward, keeping a tight hold on his harness. As they entered the elevator car, Mary couldn't help but notice the way Susan kept inching back farther into the corner of the elevator.

That's when she realized the truth.

"Are you afraid of dogs?" Mary asked her.

Susan took a deep breath, her wary gaze still on Finnegan. "I was attacked by a dog as a child and severely injured." She pulled her hair back and pointed to an ugly scar behind her right ear. "It marked me for life, both inside and out."

Mary could see the terror in her eyes, now that they were no longer shaded by anger.

"That's why I had such a strong reaction to seeing your dog in the hotel the other day," Susan continued. "I realize now that my behavior was really quite rude. I hope you'll accept my apology."

The words came out stiffly and Mary could see the reason for it was because the woman was almost paralyzed with fear.

"Lay down, Finnegan," Mary ordered, wanting the woman to feel more comfortable. The dog instantly obeyed, crossing his paws in front of him and laying his head on top of them.

Susan relaxed a little, though her back still hugged the wall. "Thank you."

The woman raised a shaky hand to brush the hair off her forehead. "I know it's ridiculous, but I just start to panic whenever I see a dog. Especially a big one like him."

Mary understood. She'd come to believe that fear explained many of the bad behaviors so rampant in society.

That didn't mean she excused rude behavior. However, she knew that understanding the reason behind that behavior was the key to diffusing uncomfortable situations.

Unfortunately, Mary knew she couldn't fix Susan's fear of dogs. The woman would probably always be afraid of them given her traumatic experience.

"My niece told me about your conversation with her the other day," Susan said, still keeping a wary eye on Finnegan. "She was fascinated by your service dog and now thinks she wants to be a trainer one day. Both you and Finnegan made a huge impression on her."

"Amanda's a delightful girl," Mary said with a smile. "If she's interested, I can put her in contact with the director of the facility that trained Finnegan."

Susan's face softened. "Would you? I'm sure Amanda would be absolutely thrilled."

Mary reached into her purse and drew out a small piece of paper. "Here's her name and e-mail address," she said, jotting it down. "The training center is located near San Francisco."

"I can't tell you how much I appreciate this," Susan said, her eyes moist. "I hope this means you forgive me for my earlier behavior toward you and Finnegan."

"Of course I forgive you," Mary said gently. She felt God's presence with them in that elevator and knew once more that He truly worked in wonderful ways.

The doors to the elevator opened and Susan looked up. "I guess this is my floor. Would you mind if I ask you more about training service dogs? I'm afraid my niece was embarrassed by my behavior the other day, too, and I want to find a way to make it up to her."

Mary followed her out into the hallway, Finnegan standing close to the wheelchair. "What do you want to know?"

Susan hesitated. "Amanda says she wants to make training service dogs her career, but she has no idea how to go about it. I was hoping you might have some advice for us."

Mary smiled, happy to help. "Maybe the three of us can get together to talk about it some more before we have to leave."

"Really?" Susan looked surprised. "You would do that after . . . everything?"

"It would be my pleasure," Mary interjected. "Just give me a call. I'm in Room 348."

"I will," Susan promised, reaching out to shake her hand. "Thank you again."

Mary watched as the woman stepped gingerly around Finnegan to avoid any contact with him. To his credit, he didn't move a muscle as Susan passed him and made her way down the hall.

Mary wheeled her chair back to the elevator and pushed the button. As the doors closed she gave the command for Finnegan to start working once more. Her heart rejoiced that she'd made the decision to leave the hotel room today and face the world again.

In return, she'd been blessed with the gift of understanding and given the gift of forgiveness.

"I think this trip was worth it after all," she told Finnegan.

CHAPTER ❀ NINETEEN

ABBY ALMOST RAN INTO her sister when she opened the door to the hotel room. "Hey, there. Where are you going?"

"They changed the time of my taping for the scrimshaw," Mary explained, rolling her wheelchair aside to let Abby into the room. "I just got the call a few minutes ago so I need to get downstairs."

Abby knew the show conducted the tapings in three different rooms to accommodate all the various segments. Unfortunately, her taping and Mary's now conflicted.

She checked her watch. "Will you be done in time to see the locket segment?"

Mary frowned. "I don't know. The woman I spoke to on the phone told me it might take up to an hour. Aren't you due at your taping soon?"

"In ten minutes," she replied, disappointed that Mary wouldn't be there with her. Abby wasn't quite sure how she'd react when Sylvia told the television world about her grandmother's locket and she wanted her sister there for support.

"I'm sorry," Mary said, reaching out to squeeze her hand. "I so wanted to be there. I'll be thinking of you though."

Abby nodded, standing at the door as her sister and Finnegan proceeded into the hallway. "And I'll be thinking of you. Good luck with the scrimshaw."

"Thanks." Mary headed to the elevator, moving more quickly than usual.

Abby sighed, then closed the door, aware she didn't have much time to get ready. She wanted to comb her hair and touch up her makeup before she appeared on camera.

Exactly ten minutes later, when Abby arrived in the Tamarack Room for the taping, she was more nervous than she'd expected. It took a while for Ned to get everything just right. At last Abby sat in front of the appraiser and waited for it all to begin.

The director flashed a sign at the cameraman, then pointed to Sylvia. She took a deep breath, then smiled at the camera.

"What we have here," Sylvia began, "is an exquisite example of the work of the renowned New York goldsmith Nigel Black."

The table was draped in plush blue velvet with her grandmother's gold locket showcased on a flocked necklace board.

One of the jewelry restorers employed by the show had polished the locket to a high sheen. Now it gleamed under the bright lights of the makeshift studio as Sylvia described in great detail some of the elements that made it so unique.

Her voice droned in Abby's ear. She was too apprehensive about what was coming next to pay attention to the remarks about the styling and metal craft.

After what seemed like forever, Sylvia looked up at Abby.

"Can you tell us something about the provenance of this locket?"

"It belonged to my grandmother, Lora Deal." Abby's voice was calm and even, despite her inner trepidation. "She traveled from New York City to Nebraska on the orphan train when she was eleven years old."

"Do you happen to know the year of her journey or how she came into possession of the locket?"

"The year was 1905, but that's about all I know. My grandmother never took the locket off, though. It was very special to her."

Sylvia nodded. "I think it's safe to assume that most orphan children did not own something this valuable, which brings us to an interesting twist to the story."

Abby held her breath, waiting for the revelation that might break her mother's heart.

"Our researchers," the appraiser continued, "have discovered that this particular locket was commissioned by a very wealthy European family living in New York City during the same year that your grandmother boarded the orphan train."

Abby's interest in the story overcame her anxiety. All the Internet stories she'd read only had the barest of details about the theft of the locket.

"Do you know if your grandmother had any connection to such a family? Perhaps as a domestic?"

Abby shook her head. "I really don't know. She never mentioned it."

"The reason I ask," the appraiser said, "is because a fire consumed several houses in a very affluent section of Manhattan. There was quite a bit of looting at these homes before they could be secured."

Abby remembered reading about a fire, though she'd read that it had been contained at the goldsmith's shop. Just another example that you couldn't trust everything you read on the Internet.

"It would be interesting to know if your grandmother had been working as a domestic at this house," Sylvia turned to the camera. "Remember that there were very lax child labor laws in this country at that time. It was not unusual for a young child to be working twelve- to fourteen-hour days."

Abby had come here for answers and only seemed to be finding more questions. Had Grandma Lora worked as a servant for a European family? Had she been in the house the night of the fire?

Sylvia turned back to Abby. "It's possible that little eleven-year-old Lora lost her job after the fire and was caught up in the sweep of orphans and neglected children shipped to the Midwest by some newly organized child welfare organizations."

Abby was aware of a growing crowd around her. The crew had cordoned off the area for taping, but many spectators could stand behind the ropes and watch the proceedings. She even saw Marcus out of the corner of her eye.

"Do you know what happened to the family?" Abby asked her.

Sylvia nodded. "None of them were injured in the fire. In fact, their house only suffered minor smoke damage. However, the locket, along with several other of their belongings, was lost forever when the looters came through. That's why I was so excited when I saw your locket."

Abby sat back in her chair, digesting the story. "But we still don't know how she got it. If she worked for the family or . . ."

"Was connected to the looters," Sylvia concluded for her. "And it's doubtful that we ever will. So much history was lost when all those children were dispersed out in the Midwest. Many of them lost contact with their remaining relatives and some didn't even retain their birth certificate, which often caused them problems later in life."

Grandma Lora had always refused to look back because it was too painful for her. Now that Abby knew about the ill mother she'd had to leave behind, Abby understood that reluctance better.

"I'm so glad you brought the locket to us today," Sylvia told her. "The orphan trains are a fascinating piece of American history and one that is often overlooked. Tell us, what became of your grandmother's journey on the orphan train? I take it she was adopted?"

Abby nodded. "Yes, by a very good family in Nebraska. They raised her as their own."

"Wonderful," she replied with a warm smile. "I always like to hear a happy ending."

Abby was grateful for the information Sylvia had given her. "Thank you for your help."

"It's my pleasure, but we're not done yet."

Some of the people around them laughed as Sylvia clasped her hands together. "Now, as to the value. Normally, a locket by Nigel Black brings about two to three thousand dollars."

There were gasps from the spectators surrounding them.

"However," Sylvia continued, "the provenance of this particular piece makes it worth about double that, so I'd value it for insurance purposes at around five thousand dollars."

Abby was stunned at the price, though she knew it would

never be sold. The locket held too much sentimental value for her family.

"And cut!" the director shouted. "That's a keeper. Good job, people."

Everyone around them began to disperse. Sylvia reached across the table to shake Abby's hand.

"Thank you so much for bringing the beautiful locket to the show. I think we got a lot of good mileage out of it. I'm always happy to teach a little history to our viewing audience during my appraisals."

As a former college professor herself, Abby knew the satisfaction such a job could give. "You're very welcome. And thank you for everything. I know my mother will appreciate it as much as I do."

The crew began bustling around them, setting the stage for the next appraisal. She saw Ned chatting with one of the other cameramen and Hans talking with one of the other appraisers on the show.

Jeffrey sped by her and Abby called out his name. "Hello, Jeffrey."

He stopped on a dime and spun around to face her. "Oh, hello there, Dr. Stanton. I didn't even see you. Are we still on for lunch?"

"I can't wait."

"Me neither," he said with a weary sigh. "Chloe's been out of commission with a bad cold for the last two days so we've been short-handed."

"Oh dear. I hope she starts feeling better soon."

"She's already promised to be back on the job by the final taping of the day, no matter how bad she feels."

Abby realized how quickly time was winding down. Tomorrow morning she'd be heading back to Sparrow Island. She hated the thought of leaving behind her catbird painting, but so far it hadn't shown up anywhere and she was no closer to cracking the case.

Someone called out Jeffrey's name from backstage.

"That's our state-of-the-art paging system," he said wryly, headed in that direction. "Just shout as loud as you can."

As she left the platform, Marcus approached her. "Congratulations on a job well done."

She smiled at him. "It was nice to see you in the audience."

"After watching that taping, I'd say you'll have one of the featured segments on the show."

"Do you really think so?"

"Absolutely," he affirmed. "It has everything to make good television. An orphan child, a fire, a wealthy family and the mystery of a valuable one-of-a-kind locket that was missing for almost a century." He moved in to take a closer look at the locket. "It is quite exquisite now that it's all polished up."

"You're not going to make me an offer for the locket are you?" she teased.

He laughed. "Not a chance. Even though I'm in the business of buying and selling antiques, I know that some things in life are priceless. Like love and family and friendship."

She was glad he understood. The sentimental value of Grandma Lora's locket far outweighed its monetary value. Abby just wished she knew why it had been so very special to her grandmother.

Perhaps the fact that it contained a lock of her mother's hair had been enough of a reason.

"There's your sister," Marcus said as Mary hailed them.

They met her in a secluded corner of the ballroom, away from the chaos of the multiple taping segments occurring throughout the room.

"How did it go?" Mary asked.

"Very interesting." Abby replied, then told her the story behind Grandma Lora's locket. "And what about your scrimshaw appraisal?"

Mary smiled. "The appraiser was fascinated by it and suggested that a Boston museum with a special whaling wing might be interested in displaying it. That might be a solution to my problem of deciding which of my children should have the tooth."

"I think both Nancy and Zack would be thrilled to see one of Jacob's treasures in a museum," Abby told her.

"So do I," Mary agreed, then looked at Marcus. "And are you having a good time this week, Mr. Wolfe?"

"Splendid," he replied, "but it would be even better if you called me Marcus."

Mary's smile widened. "All right, Marcus."

Abby glanced at her watch, knowing she didn't have much time before meeting Jeffrey for his short break. "Did you have a chance to talk to Betty?"

"I did," Mary signaled for Finnegan to sit down beside her wheelchair. "That's what I wanted to talk to you about."

"Betty Carstens?" Marcus said. "Isn't she the woman whose teapot was stolen?"

"Yes," Abby replied. "Her sister Thelma is from Sparrow Island."

"Betty told me all the details." Mary said. "She still feels horribly guilty for not hiding the teapot. She said with the rush of arriving late to the hotel, then changing rooms at the last moment, and the anxiety of seeing her sister again after so many years—"

"Changing rooms?" Abby interjected, intrigued by this new fact. "When did that happen?"

"Shortly after she checked into the hotel," Mary said. "She said her first room reeked of smoke and that she'd specifically requested a nonsmoking room when she made her reservations because she has bad allergies."

That blew Abby's theory that the thief had lurked by the front desk and overheard Betty's room number when she checked in.

It also meant that the room number Thelma had given for Betty during the preliminary evaluation had been incorrect. So the crew of *Antique Adventures* had the wrong hotel room number as well, weakening the possibility that one of them had stolen the teapot.

"What is it?" Marcus asked, gazing into her face, "I can almost see the wheels turning inside that head of yours."

She smiled, his words breaking her concentration. "I'm still trying to solve this theft case. It has me more than a bit baffled."

"Well, I admire your tenacity," Marcus said. "I'd have thought you'd have given up by now."

Mary chuckled. "My sister doesn't give up easily, Marcus. Once she sets her mind to solving a problem, she's usually successful."

"Looks like I'm running behind again," Abby said, checking her watch. "I'm supposed to be meeting Jeffrey for lunch and I don't want to be late. He has so little time for his break."

"Have fun," Mary told her, then rolled her wheelchair

closer to the action so she could get a good seat for the next taping segment.

Marcus walked with Abby to the doors of the ballroom. "You're a fascinating woman, Abigail Stanton."

"And usually much more punctual," she said, pausing beside him.

He opened the door for her. "I hope we can see more of each other when we return to the San Juan Islands." Then he picked up her hand and kissed the top of it. "Au revoir, my dear Abby."

CHAPTER ✿ TWENTY

ABBY'S HAND STILL
tingled when she reached the small café on the main floor of
the hotel. Jeffrey sat at a round table, his soda cup and a deli
sandwich already in front of him.

"I'm so sorry I'm late," Abby said, taking the empty chair
across from him.

"No problem." Jeffrey took a sip from his straw. "I went
ahead and started without you, since I only have a few minutes
for my break."

"I'm glad we could squeeze in a little time togther." Abby
ordered a salad and a cup of green tea from a passing waiter.
"You looked pretty frazzled earlier."

Jeffrey leaned back in his chair. "I'm exhausted. It's been
pretty chaotic around here with Chloe out of the picture.
Dr. Houston is completely lost without her. In fact, this is his
last show. He announced today that he's going to retire."

That came as a surprise to Abby. "What brought this on?"

Jeffrey shrugged. "I think he's tired of looking over his shoulder, waiting for someone to point out another mistake. As much as I like the man, I have to admit that his work has gotten sloppy over the last year or so."

The waiter set Abby's tea in front of her. "Maybe he's just tired. The pace is amazing. I'm especially impressed by all the research the appraisers do."

"You have to remember they have several research assistants to help them out. Once we provide them the final list of items that will appear on the show, they set to work finding out as much information about the item as they can."

Research assistants. Abby hadn't even considered them as possible suspects. They'd have all the information necessary to perpetrate the crime. She sank back in her chair, feeling more overwhelmed than ever.

Jeffrey took another sip of his soda. "I always learn something new with each show, that's for sure. For instance, there's some evidence that Audubon did paint a gray catbird during his early years."

Abby blinked. "So the show did research on my painting even though it's still missing?"

"We sure did," Jeffrey replied. "There's a good chance your painting will mysteriously reappear before we wrap up taping, if what's happened in the past is any indication."

Abby admired his optimism, but she wasn't holding out much hope. "Even if I do get the painting back in time, I wouldn't want to bump somebody else off who'd been moved to my spot from the waiting list."

"There's no bumping," Jeffrey assured her. "We just edit down to the bare bones so we can fit everybody in." Then he grinned at her. "Although I doubt there will be much editing with that locket segment you just did. Everybody I talked to said it rocked."

She'd been around college kids enough to know that he'd just given her a compliment. "Thank you. I thought so too."

The alarm went off on Jeffrey's watch and he grimaced at the noise. "That means my break's over."

"It seems like we just got here."

"I know. My break was shortened to fifteen minutes because of Chloe's illness." Then he slapped himself in the forehead. "I can't believe I just sat here with you and didn't mention birds even one time."

She laughed. "That's because you're immersed in your work. It's easy to see you like your job, Jeffrey, even if it isn't in the field of ornithology."

"I guess you're right," he admitted, then rose from his chair. "See you around, Dr. Stanton."

She sat at the table and watched Jeffrey jog toward the ball-room. Then she took a sip of her tea and thought about the investigation. She, too, had been immersed, just as Jeffrey was in his work. Abby wondered if it was time to step back and look at this case from a whole new angle.

Before she could ponder that thought further, Bill Briley showed up at her table. The hotel detective grabbed a chair, straddling it as he sat down across from her.

"I've got something," Briley announced, grabbing a potato chip from Jeffrey's plate.

Abby waited for him to continue. She'd grown used to his abrupt manner, even if she did question some of his interrogation techniques.

"That tea set belonging to those Rogers sisters is worth a bundle," he said.

"How do you know?"

He arched a brow. "I'm a digger, Dr. Stanton. I keep digging until I find a gold nugget. And this nugget is solid gold. In fact, it's worth about twenty thousand dollars."

Her jaw dropped. "The tea set is worth twenty thousand dollars? Are you sure?"

He nodded. "I found an identical English teapot that had been up for auction at Sotheby's two years ago. It went for ten thousand bucks, but the listing said the complete set would have gone for twice that much."

More people crowded into the busy café, the hotel lobby buzzing with people now that the noon hour had arrived. She found herself wondering where they'd all come from and where they'd go after the show was over. One of them could even be the thief and she wouldn't know it.

"Dr. Stanton?"

She looked up to see Briley staring quizzically at her and Abby realized she hadn't heard a word that he'd been saying. The long week was catching up with her and she reached for her tea and took a sip. It was lukewarm now, but still soothing.

"I'm sorry, Mr. Briley. Please go on."

He scowled at her. "As I was saying, with this new information about the value of the stolen teapot, it turns out this heist was worth quite a bundle. That ups the ante in my book."

"Does that mean you think we should call in the police now? That they'll take the thefts more seriously?"

He shrugged. "Well, it's definitely a felony. Grand larceny. Two counts, if your bird painting's worth anything."

Abby still didn't know for certain what her catbird was worth. According to Jeffrey, there were rumors in the art world that Audubon had painted a gray catbird early in his career, but there was no proof she had it.

"So what's your next move?" Abby inquired, almost afraid to find out.

He reached for the last chip on the plate. "To tell you the truth, I'm stumped at this point. I finished checking out the rest of your Sparrow Island gang and most of them are clean."

She breathed a sigh of relief and barely resisted the urge to say, "I told you so."

He popped the chip into his mouth, then pulled the small notepad from his pocket. "I'll run the info by you just to see if anything stands out."

Abby opened her mouth to tell him it wasn't necessary, but he barreled ahead, oblivious to anything she might have to say.

He flipped over a page and scanned his unique shorthand. "Hugo Baron. This guy's a real do-gooder. I couldn't find anything negative about him, which seems a little suspicious in and of itself."

Abby sat back and folded her arms across her chest. Briley almost seemed disappointed that her friends weren't felons.

He moved on to the next page in his notebook. "Mary Reynolds."

She sat up. "That's my sister."

"I know. I think I mentioned before that one of my first rules of investigative work is to look at the people closest to the victim."

Abby couldn't believe he was serious. "But you can eliminate her immediately. Finnegan wouldn't have started barking like that if Mary was the one in the hotel room."

"I know," he admitted, "that's why I decided to cross her off the list fairly early in the investigation. Same with Thelma Rogers. She was almost more upset about the stolen teapot than her sister."

"Why do you say that?"

Briley shrugged. "I questioned them together. Thelma kept crying about it and Betty kept handing her tissue after tissue. Before long they were both crying so much I had to end the interview." He rolled his eyes toward the ceiling. "Women."

Abby was surprised a hard-boiled ex-cop like Briley could be so easily disconcerted by tears. "What else do you have?"

He flipped through his notepad, then shook his head. "That's it."

"So all of my Sparrow Island friends are now free of suspicion?"

"I guess so." He jammed the notepad back into his shirt pocket. "I thought we had some good leads there for a while, but they all turned cold."

She just hoped her friends would forgive her after their privacy had been invaded by Briley's methods. "So are you finally ready to admit the thief is most likely someone connected to the *Antique Adventures* show?"

"Not quite yet," Briley told her. Then he looked around for a waiter and shouted an order of a cup of black coffee. "Those chips were really salty."

"What other suspects could you possibly have in mind?" Abby pushed her teacup away. "Especially when you know about the prior incidents in other cities?"

He met her gaze. "Your new flame, Marcus Wolfe, to name just one."

Abby blushed. "I'd hardly call him my flame. He's just a new friend."

"Do all of your friends go around kissing your hand like I saw him do just a short while ago?"

Abby briefly wondered if Briley had been following her, then dismissed the idea. It was more likely he'd been following Marcus if he now considered him a suspect. She had to admit to having a few suspicions about him herself, given the circumstances.

"That hand kiss was more than a friendly farewell," Briley continued. "Guys around here just don't do that sort of thing. At least, not any of the guys I know."

Abby wondered if he considered that suspicious behavior. "I thought it was quite a lovely gesture, actually. Perhaps more men should adopt it."

He snorted. "Not likely." Then he frowned over at the barista counter. "Where's that waiter with my coffee? I don't have time to sit around here all day."

Neither did Abby, so she wanted Briley to get to the point a quickly as possible. "Tell me why you suspect Marcus."

"The usual reasons—means, motive and opportunity. He knew your room number and the fact that your painting was there." Briley held up the index finger of his right hand. "That takes care of the first one—the means."

"And his motive?"

"To sell it, of course. The man is in the business, so that's a no-brainer. He could probably find a buyer in a New York minute."

"That takes care of two of your criteria." Abby folded her hands on the table. "And the third one?"

"The third aspect of the crime is opportunity. As far as I know, Wolfe didn't have a solid alibi at the time of either crime."

Abby wished she could counter his arguments, but they were all true. Marcus did have the means, motive and opportunity. She just didn't believe that he was guilty of the thefts.

Or she didn't want to believe it.

"What's wrong?" he challenged. "I expected you to tell me all the reasons why Wolfe is innocent, yet you aren't saying a word."

Abby realized that she wanted to argue with Briley just because she didn't care for his manner or investigative techniques.

Step away, she reminded herself, trying to separate the facts from her emotions. *Look at the situation objectively.*

"You make some good points," Abby said at last. "But I believe you should still have some actual proof before you accuse Marcus of anything."

"I agree," he replied.

That took her by surprise. Abby didn't think she and Briley had agreed on anything since they'd met.

"That's why," he continued, "I'm having one of the maid's search Wolfe's room as we speak."

"You're what?" she said, aghast. "That can't be legal without a search warrant, can it?"

"We don't have time to bother with the legal technicalities, so I just slipped her a twenty and asked her to take a good, hard look for your bird painting and the teapot in there while she was cleaning up this morning. If she finds them, then the case will be solved."

Abby wanted to warn Marcus, but she didn't know where he was or how to reach him. The maid would be in and out of his room before she could contact him.

"You may not like my methods," Briley said, gauging the expression on her face, "but I get results, Dr. Stanton. Sometimes you have to bend the rules a little bit to win the game."

Abby didn't agree, but she knew it wouldn't do any good to try and convince Briley. He was too set in his ways. She would try to find Marcus and inform him about the situation, since she was appalled that the hotel detective would invade the man's hotel room and his privacy without any kind of warning.

"I don't think that waiter is ever coming back," Briley grumbled. He reached for her tea cup. "Are you going to finish this?"

"No," she replied, eager to be on her way. "You go ahead."

He tipped up the cup and emptied it in one long gulp. "Good stuff. I wonder if it would taste any better out of a ten-thousand-dollar teapot."

Briley set the cup on the table. "I guess we'd have to find that buyer at Sotheby's to find out."

He reached for a napkin and wiped his mouth. "I can tell you this much. If I was that Carstens woman, I would have sold that ten thousand dollar teapot a long time ago, before anyone had a chance to steal it. Think of all that beautiful cash down the drain."

His words brought the image of rain water flowing into a sewer drain. Then she thought about the hurricane Betty had lived through two years ago and the torrential downpours that had caused so much damage to her home.

Step back.

Abby stared at him as a thought suddenly hit her. *Is it possible?*

"Are you okay, doc?" Briley asked, his voice edged with concern. "You're looking a little peaked."

Why haven't I considered this before? she thought.

Abby realized she was gripping the edge of the table. She relaxed her hands and let go. "Yes, I'm fine, thank you."

"If you didn't want me to finish your tea, you should have just said something," he grumbled, misreading her reaction. "I was so parched I just couldn't stand it anymore."

"I didn't mind at all," she assured him. Especially since Bill Briley might have just given her the key to finding the missing teapot.

CHAPTER ❧ TWENTY-ONE

ABBY FOUND THELMA and Betty in the hotel courtyard.

She'd tracked them down through Hugo, who had informed her that the sisters were having tea and crumpets together before their taping.

Antique Adventures still wanted the sisters on the air, even with only half of the original English tea set. They were scheduled for the last segment of the afternoon and had spent most of the morning in the hotel's beauty salon having their hair and nails done.

"I hope I'm not interrupting," Abby said as she approached their table.

"Not at all," Thelma replied. "Pull up a chair and join us."

Abby found a white patio chair nearby and placed it near the sisters. She almost hated to intrude on their peaceful tea, but this simply couldn't wait. She had to know if she was right.

"How did your taping segment go, Abby?" Thelma asked, setting down her cup.

"Very well," Abby replied. "Although I was a little more nervous than I thought I'd be."

"I'm petrified," Betty confessed, kneading her thin hands together. "I've never been on television before, unless you count all those news cameras after the hurricane."

"You'll do fine," Thelma assured her sister. "All you have to do is follow my lead. I know everything there is to know about Mama's tea set."

"I'm not sure that's true," Abby said gently.

Thelma looked at her. "What do you mean?"

Abby turned to Betty. "You love Thelma, don't you?"

Betty's brow wrinkled in confusion. "Of course I do. I always have."

"In fact, you love her so much you'll do almost anything to protect her from getting hurt." Abby took a deep breath. "You'll even lie."

Thelma's eyes blazed with indignation. "Abigail Stanton! How could you say such a thing about my own sister? Why, you've never even met Betty before this week. You don't know anything about her."

Abby didn't respond, letting Thelma's anger flare out. She just kept looking at Betty, calling her bluff. It didn't take long for the woman to fold.

"How did you figure it out?" Betty asked, her voice barely a whisper.

"It wasn't easy, but there were a few clues," Abby told her. "Like the fact that you changed rooms on that first day, so it would be almost impossible for a thief to know your new room number—especially if it was someone connected with *Antique Adventures*. Thelma would have given them the number of your first hotel room during the evaluation. The one you never stayed in."

Thelma started sputtering beside them. "What is she talking about Betty?"

Her sister's face crumpled. "Oh, Thelma."

"Then there was the fact that a teapot sold by Sotheby's two years ago is an identical match to the one you claimed was stolen." Abby knew she had to get it all out, however painful it was for both of them to hear.

Thelma turned to her sister. "Betty, please tell me what's going on."

Betty bit her lip. "I never wanted you to find out, Thelma. We hadn't spoken in ten years and I had no reason to believe we'd ever see each other again. I was desperate for money and—" Her voice broke off in a sob.

Thelma turned to Abby. "Someone please tell me what's happening here!"

"Your mother's English teapot wasn't stolen from Betty's hotel room," Abby said softly, "because she never brought it to Seattle with her in the first place."

"Of course she did," Thelma retorted. "We planned it all out a month ago. She'd bring the teapot and I'd bring the cups and saucers."

Betty slid her hands over her eyes, then wiped the tears away. "I was so thrilled when you called me about getting together, Thelma. And so terrified about what you'd think of me when you found out the truth. I was going to tell you, but I kept putting it off."

Thelma stared at her sister. Her face was pale, despite the bright glare of the sun.

"I wasn't even going to come," Betty continued. "I missed

my flight on purpose, but when you insisted I come, I just didn't have the heart to refuse. I wanted to see you again, Thelma. I wanted it so much that I lied to you."

"You did worse than lie." Thelma's tone was dull and flat. "You sold Mama's teapot."

Betty's eyes welled again as she nodded in affirmation. "Yes. I had to sell it. I was desperate for money to save my house. The last hurricane caused so much damage that I fell behind on my mortgage payments. Mama's teapot helped me save my home."

Thelma didn't say anything, she just stared straight ahead.

"Please forgive me," Betty pleaded. "I know I should have told you right away, Thelma. I was working up the courage, but when I heard about the stolen bird painting, it seemed like such an easy way to avoid causing any more problems between us."

Abby swallowed a sigh, knowing the easiest way usually wasn't the best way.

"I regretted the lie immediately," Betty confessed. "But it just kept growing bigger and bigger. Soon I was lying not only to you, but to your friends and that hotel detective. I didn't know how to stop it."

"How about by telling the truth?" Thelma challenged. "You were about to go on a national television program and lie to the entire country! With me there sitting right next to you."

Betty buried her face in her hands, sobbing now. Abby couldn't help but feel sorry for the woman. She'd made some poor decisions, but looked truly repentant.

"God hates a lying tongue," Thelma snapped, paraphrasing a verse from the sixth chapter of the book of Proverbs.

Abby had always believed God's word should be used for

guidance and support, not as a weapon in a disagreement. She opened her mouth to say something, but Thelma had already stormed off.

"What have I done?" Betty whispered, her eyes red and swollen. "Thelma will never forgive me now."

"Give her time," Abby advised. "It came as a shock to her. That tea set was so important to her."

"I know." Betty wiped away her tears. "I'm glad the truth finally came out. I'd planned to tell her, but I know now I would have just chickened out again, or worse, run back to Florida without her even knowing what really happened."

They sat in silence for a few moments, the gentle breeze drying the tears on Betty's face.

"What are you going to do now?" Abby asked her.

"Pray," Betty replied, then looked up at her. "Will you pray with me?"

"Of course," Abby reached for her hand and Betty's fingers curled tightly around it.

The two women prayed together, asking God for forgiveness and seeking peace and understanding. They prayed for Thelma and for Betty and for families everywhere who suffered from grief and discord.

The pain of losing their mother had torn Thelma and Betty apart. The rift between them had stretched for ten long years. It was finally time for the healing to begin.

CHAPTER ❦ TWENTY-TWO

ABBY SLIPPED OFF HER shoes, relieved to finally be in her hotel room after such a long day. She'd already told Mary about her encounter with Betty and Thelma. Her sister agreed that Abby had done the right thing.

"The truth had to come out," Mary said, as she stroked a brush over the golden fur on Finnegan's back. She'd removed the blue service cape and harness to groom him. The dog loved to be brushed and stood unmoving by her wheelchair.

"I just hope it's not too late for them to repair the damage." Abby sighed. "Let's never allow something like that to come between us, Mary."

"We won't," her sister vowed. "Just like I know the scrimshaw won't ever cause a rift between my son and daughter."

"So you've decided to donate it to the museum?"

She nodded. "I called both Nancy and Zack today and talked to them about it. They each thought it was a wonderful idea and a fitting tribute to their father. I have to admit I was relieved."

"You raised good children," Abby told her. "I wouldn't have expected anything different from them."

Mary smiled. "Spoken like a devoted aunt."

Abby leaned her head back against the chair. "So what shall we do for dinner tonight? Is the Sparrow Island group getting together again?"

Mary didn't say anything as she kept running the brush over Finnegan.

Abby sat up. "What's wrong?"

Her sister met her gaze. "I didn't want to mention it, because I'm sure it will all blow over soon."

"Some of them are still upset about the investigation," Abby said, already well aware of the reason for the cold shoulder from some of her friends.

Even though Briley claimed that he'd cleared all of them from suspicion, she still wasn't certain he'd stop harassing them. That was one of the reasons she'd left him a message summarizing the fate of the teapot so he could drop that part of the investigation.

"They don't really blame you," Mary explained, "but they also don't feel like you've done anything to stop Mr. Briley. He's just bulldozing through their lives, uncovering private details, as if he doesn't care who he hurts in the process."

"He doesn't care," Abby said bluntly. "And I've tried to stop him. He won't listen to me."

"I know." Mary ran the brush down Finnegan's front legs. "Feelings are still a bit bruised, though. They're going to take some time to heal."

"I wish there was something I could do."

Mary set the brush down. "I'm afraid the news that the

teapot wasn't actually stolen won't make them feel any better. At least they knew that had substantial value."

"And I only paid ten dollars for my catbird painting," Abby said. "They're right, in a way. It hardly seems worth all the trouble it's caused."

"It's not your fault," Mary assured her. "You can't control Mr. Briley and you can't be blamed for wanting to get your painting back. What it's worth isn't the issue. The painting belongs to you."

Abby wasn't sorry for her investigation into the theft, but she did feel badly that her friends had been swept into it and hurt along the way. She wished she could think of some way to make it up to them.

"All finished," Mary said, attaching the service cape and harness on Finnegan once more. "He's dressed and ready for duty. Would you like to join us for a long walk? We should see something of Seattle before we leave for home tomorrow."

The idea appealed to Abby. "I'm all for it. Just give me a few minutes to change."

She walked over to the closet and retrieved a pair of blue jeans.

"Not those," Mary said, shaking her head at her sister's choice. "Pick something a little nicer."

Abby studied her sister. "Why do I get the feeling that you've got something up your sleeve?"

Mary's mouth turned up in a grin. "I think we should call Marcus and ask him to join us. That seems like a good reason to wear something extra special."

Abby blushed. "I don't know if he—"

Her words were cut short by a knock at the door.

Mary glanced at her. "Were you expecting anyone?"

Abby shook her head. "No. You?"

"No." Mary rolled her wheelchair over to the door and opened it.

Bill Briley stood on the other side. "Good afternoon, ladies."

Abby walked over to the door. "This is a surprise, Mr. Briley."

He nodded. "I'm sure it is. Now brace yourself for an even bigger surprise."

He stepped away from the door, then returned holding the gray catbird painting in his hands. "Look what I found."

Abby's mouth dropped open in shock. She'd almost given up hope of ever seeing it again. "My catbird! Where did you find it?"

"Exactly where I thought I would," he replied, handing it over to her. "In Marcus Wolfe's room."

"What?" Mary gasped. "That can't be true."

"It is," Briley assured her. "The maid found it on his closet shelf. It was in plain view as soon as she opened the door. That shows some arrogance, doesn't it? I guess guys like Wolfe think they're too smart to ever get caught."

Abby carefully set the painting on top of her bed, still reeling from the revelation that Marcus had taken it. "What about the quilt?"

"What quilt?" Briley asked.

"The picture was wrapped in an old family quilt," Mary informed him. "Did you find it in Marcus's room too?"

Briley shook his head. "Just the picture. He probably disposed of the quilt as soon as he took it."

Abby would be very surprised if he'd thrown it out. He'd admired the quilt when he'd first seen it Monday on the

Victoria Clipper. But maybe that had been a lie. Maybe every-thing about him had been a lie.

She felt a little sick inside.

Briley looked quizzically at Abby. "I thought you'd be more excited."

"Oh, I am excited." Abby ran her fingers over the gilt frame. "It just comes as quite a shock."

"Don't feel too bad," he told her. "You're not the first woman to be duped by a smooth talker and you won't be the last."

"She wasn't duped," Mary protested.

"Wolfe's last name fits him perfectly," Briley continued as if Mary hadn't spoken. "He saw his prey and went after it. Then he gets his kicks romancing the victim while he's got your bird painting stashed in his hotel room closet. That takes some nerve."

That image he drew of her friendship with Marcus gave Abby a bad taste in her mouth. And she still wasn't completely convinced it was true. Even with the evidence right in front of her. "So what happens now?"

"The police already investigated the scene," Briley said. "I called them as soon as I found the painting in Wolfe's room. They released the painting to me when I explained that you needed it for the show." He puffed out his chest. "It sure doesn't hurt to have connections in the department."

"And Marcus?" Abby said.

"The cops are looking for him as we speak. I'm sure an arrest is imminent. They'll probably want a statement from you eventually."

Abby nodded, feeling strangely numb.

Mary moved toward her. "Are you all right?"

"Yes," she replied, not wanting to worry her sister. Either the reality of the situation hadn't hit Abby yet or she just wasn't ready to accept that Marcus was a thief. She'd always thought of herself as a good judge of character.

"Well, I've done my good deed for the day," Briley said, moving toward the door. "Another case solved. I'm sure the manager will be thrilled." He grinned. "Might even earn me a bonus."

Mary turned to her after Briley left. "Oh, Abby, I'm so sorry. I can't believe Marcus would do something like this."

"Neither can I." Abby admitted. "But it's hard to argue with the facts right in front of us. Briley told me he was sending someone into Marcus's room to search it. I thought it would be just another dead end."

"At least you found out now," Mary said, placing a comforting hand on her shoulder. "Before your friendship with him went any further."

Abby looked up at her. "Do you mind if I skip the walk? I'm not feeling up to it now."

"Of course not," Mary replied. "I'm skipping it too. We've go something more important to do."

"What's that?"

Mary picked up the bird painting. "They're still taping the show. Let's go down to the ballroom and see if they can fit you into the schedule. That's why you came to Seattle, isn't it?"

She had a point. If nothing else it would take Abby's mind off the fact that Marcus was about to be arrested.

"I'll call Jeffrey," Abby said, reaching for her cell phone, "and see if they still have a spot open. I don't even care if I get on the show, I just want to know if the appraiser thinks this is a real Audubon."

"Marcus must have thought so," Mary said, grabbing her bag off the table. "Why else would he have taken your painting?"

That was a question Abby still couldn't answer. Why would Marcus take it, then pursue a friendship with her? Despite what Briley had said, she just didn't think he was the type of man to play those kinds of games.

Then she remembered their conversation on the *Victoria Clipper* and his words echoed in her mind. *I just like to take a gamble every now and then.*

Abby knew she might be wrong about him, but every instinct told her Marcus wasn't a thief. Which meant that someone else had planted the bird painting in his room to make him look guilty.

Now it was Abby's turn to take a gamble that she was right.

CHAPTER ❦ TWENTY-THREE

D R. WESLEY HOUSTON welcomed Abby onto the stage with a warm smile. "I see you've brought a fine portrait of a bird for us today."

Abby was still trying to catch her breath. By the time she and Mary reached Jeffrey to tell him her painting had been recovered, the last taping segment of the day was almost over.

Jeffrey had hurried Abby through the backstage area, shouting orders to the production crew and reassuring her that they would be able to edit any extra material later if they went overtime.

Mary and Finnegan stayed out on the floor, lending their support with the rest of the crowd gathered around the display table.

"What can you tell me about your item?" Dr. Houston asked her.

"This is a painting of a gray catbird," Abby explained, "which is a bird indigenous to most of North America. They prefer wild fruit for their diet and most commonly migrate along the coast of North Carolina as well as Florida and Louisiana."

Dr. Houston turned to face the camera. "We are very fortunate to have an expert here with us. Dr. Stanton is an ornithologist and Associate Curator at the Sparrow Island Nature Conservatory in the beautiful San Juan Islands."

Abby wanted to hug him for giving a free plug to the conservatory. They relied on tourists and contributions to keep it growing and relished all the publicity they could get.

"Since you're an ornithologist, this is too good an opportunity to pass up," Dr. Houston continued. "I've always wanted to know where the expression 'sitting in the catbird seat' came from. Do you have any idea, Dr. Stanton?"

Abby smiled, glad she knew the answer to this one. "Well, the male Australian catbird is part of the Ptilonorhynchidae family and is known for building a very colorful and high nest to attract a mate. In fact, he'll often use hundreds of artfully arranged rocks and seashells for the female to sit atop her throne."

Dr. Houston smiled. "So that's why the phrase denotes a position of honor or envy."

"Exactly," Abby replied, "I believe the actual phrase you mentioned originated from a humorous short story by James Thurber called *The Catbird Seat*, although there is some dispute about it"

Dr. Houston nodded. "That's something that I'm sure our viewers will enjoy researching for themselves."

Abby began to grow warm under the bright lights. She could see Hugo standing by her sister in the audience. It pained her to realize Marcus was probably on his way to the police station right now.

Dr. Houston picked up a white conductor's baton off the table to use as a pointer. "Now let's examine this particular catbird and see if Dr. Stanton will be sitting in the catbird seat when I complete my appraisal."

Abby smiled. "I should point out that this gray catbird is an American bird that is unrelated to the Australian catbird and belongs to a different family called Mimidae."

"An important clarification," Dr. Houston observed. "Do you believe this painting is an accurate depiction of a gray catbird?"

"Very much so," Abby replied. "It seems so real to me that it looks like it could fly off the canvas. That's one of the reasons I enjoy it so much."

He nodded. "It truly is a quite lovely example of American art in the early to mid-nineteenth century. Where did you buy it?"

"At a flea market," she replied. "I saw it among a stack of other pictures and fell in love with it right away."

He chuckled. "So this is one of those flea market finds that we so enjoy hearing about on *Antique Adventures*. Would you mind telling us how much you paid for it?"

"Ten dollars."

Someone in the audience gasped, then she could hear murmuring behind her. Jeffrey hurried out there to silence the talkers.

"Which just goes to show once again," Dr. Houston opined, "that there are always hidden treasures among the trash. You have a good eye for art, Dr. Stanton. Now shall we get on with the appraisal?"

"Please," Abby said, her heart starting to beat a little faster.

He grasped the corner of the frame with one hand, his baton in the other. "Let's start with the frame. It appears to be original, although it is not of the best quality. There are some chips and dents and a few other damage issues. But considering that this frame is almost two hundred years old, it has survived quite nicely."

Abby glanced at her sister and Hugo, who gave her encouraging smiles. She was very hopeful that it was an Audubon, given Dr. Houston's barely concealed excitement about it, but she would treasure the painting however the appraisal turned out. She was just so happy and relieved to have it back in her possession.

"Now we'll move on to the painting itself." Dr. Houston carefully leaned the painting back on the sturdy metal picture stand. "The brush strokes are somewhat primitive, although there's a wonderful use of color. You can see the vibrant burst of rusty red underneath the tail feathers and the gradual movement of the gray to black variegation on the wings. It really is quite impressive work."

Abby reminded herself to breathe as Dr. Houston turned to her with a twinkle in his blue eyes.

"Now for the best part," he continued. "It's often difficult to ascertain whether a painting by a famous artist is an original or a copy. We consider several factors, including the age of the canvas, if the picture is signed or not, and whether or not the frame is original."

Her heart was pounding so loud she could hear it reverberate against her eardrums.

Dr. Houston picked up the magnifying glass on the table. "I have to admit that when I first saw this painting I was quite excited."

She tensed as he leaned in closer to the canvas, eyeing it through the glass.

"I am quite certain," Dr. Houston, proclaimed, "that this painting is one of the earliest works of the famous bird artist John J. Auda—" His voice faltered as he stumbled back from the painting.

Abby reached out a hand to steady him. "Dr. Houston, are you all right?"

"It can't be," he gasped. "Not again. Please, not again."

Abby waited, noting the concerned looks of the crew.

"Cut," the director yelled.

The cameras turned off and rolled back from the set as Jeffrey approached the table. "What seems to be the problem, Dr. Houston?"

The elderly appraiser stepped back from the painting, his face flushed. "I seem to have made another . . . mistake. I don't know how it's possible. I was so sure at the evaluation that this was the real thing."

Jeffrey threw an apologetic glance at Abby. "So it's not a painting by John J. Audubon?"

"No," Dr. Houston croaked. "It's a mimic. An almost perfect fake, but a fake nonetheless."

Disappointment trickled through Abby. "Are you sure?"

"Quite sure, I'm afraid." Dr. Houston sighed. "I can't believe I didn't catch it the first time. Everyone's always trying to hurry me along. Appraisal is an art much more than a science. You can't run it like an assembly line."

Jeffrey looked as if he took the criticism personally. "I understand you're upset, Dr. Houston, but we have to keep to our schedule to make the show work."

"I know, I know," the elderly man muttered. "I've heard you say it a million times."

"Okay, people, let's wrap this up. The show's over."

The crew began to disassemble the set as Jeffrey ushered Abby aside. "I'm sorry, Dr. Stanton. We won't be able to air this segment after all. Dr. Houston's in no shape to continue and it's getting late."

"I understand," she told him, patting his arm. "Don't worry about it, Jeffrey. I'm fine."

Relief flashed across his face that she wasn't upset with him. "You're the greatest, Dr. Stanton."

When one of the producers shouted his name, Jeffrey hurried over to answer the call.

Abby walked over to pick up her painting from the table, then saw Dr. Houston approaching her. His lined face looked haggard and she saw shadows of doubt and disappointment clouding his blue eyes.

"I owe you an apology, Dr. Stanton." Dr. Houston frowned at the painting in her hands. "My pride has kept me from retiring when it's become obvious to everyone else that I'm no longer up to the job."

She heard the defeat in his voice and her heart went out to him. "I have no hard feelings, Dr. Houston, believe me."

"You should," he countered, "I made you believe you had a genuine Audubon in your possession, only to disappoint you." He sighed. "I'm glad this will be my last show. I refuse to perform substandard work."

In Abby's opinion, the man was being much too hard on himself. Perfection was impossible to obtain no matter what your profession. She'd certainly made plenty of mistakes in her career. Mistakes that had ultimately led to her growth as a professional.

Abby wanted to show Dr. Houston that she still believed in him.

"This may not be an Audubon," she said, placing the cat-bird painting back on the picture stand, "but can you tell me how old it is and who might have painted it?"

"Not old at all," he replied. "The frame is old, but see this here," his pointer touched one corner of the canvas. "It's been made to look aged, but—"

He frowned, lifting up his baton and staring at the tip.

"What is it?" Abby asked him.

"Paint," he replied, rubbing the tip of his pointer with his index finger. "Fresh oil paint."

"How's that possible? I bought this painting months ago."

"It's not possible, unless . . ." His words trailed off as com-prehension dawned in his eyes.

Dr. Houston pulled a pocket knife and out of his pocket. Then he opened it and slipped the thin blade partially into the canvas. When he removed it again, a film of wet gray paint covered it.

"I wasn't wrong," he exclaimed, his voice shaking with excitement. "This is a fake, all right, but it was painted within the last day or two. The skin had dried over the surface, but the layers underneath are still wet!"

Abby felt a little dizzy from the rollercoaster of emotions she'd been riding for the last hour. Her disappointment van-ished and a thrilling curiosity took its place. "So this isn't my catbird painting?"

"No," he cried. "It's a different one. An excellent forgery, but not good enough to fool me!"

A strange feeling enveloped her as the pieces to the puzzle began to fall together. She didn't have them all yet, but she knew where to find them.

She turned to look for Mary and Hugo, surprised to find them right behind her. "Did you hear? This isn't the same painting I brought with me from home."

Hugo looked as shocked as she felt. "Amazing."

"Where did it come from?" Mary asked. "And how did it end up in Marcus' closet?"

There were so many questions, but Abby didn't have the answers.

When Dr. Houston shouted for Jeffrey, Abby saw her former student trot over to them.

"Hey," he said, looking a little frazzled around the edges, "what's going on?"

"I'll tell you what's going on," Dr. Houston said with a new air of confidence about him. "We need to finish filming the segment with Dr. Stanton. This is not the same catbird painting that I evaluated on Monday."

Sympathy softened Jeffrey's features. "I know you may want to believe that, but—"

"Look here," Dr. Houston commanded. He touched the tip of his baton to the canvas and showed it to Jeffrey. "Fresh paint."

Jeffrey's bearded jaw dropped. "You're right."

"Whoever stole Dr. Stanton's bird painting tried to replace it with this fake," Dr. Houston announced. "They even put it in the same frame. She had a true Audubon."

That news might have thrilled Abby if the real painting wasn't still missing. She stared at the fake in front of her, something niggling at her brain. Something about the colors."

"Now, now," Dr. Houston chided, breaking her reverie, "don't look so serious, Dr. Stanton. I know this all comes as quite a shock, but I've got just the thing to cheer you up. I'm having a little get-together to celebrate my retirement and I'd like you to be my special guest."

"I won't take no for an answer," Dr. Houston insisted. "I want to see you in my room, Suite 940, at seven o'clock sharp. And you're more than welcome to bring a guest with you."

Abby nodded as she reached out to touch the painting, running one finger over the red feathers under the tail of the catbird. Then she looked down at her hand, rubbing the oily red smudge between her thumb and forefinger. That's when it all began to fall into place.

CHAPTER ❦ TWENTY-FOUR

THAT EVENING, ABBY entered Dr. Houston's suite to find a small crowd gathered. She'd asked Mary to come with her, but her sister already had plans to dine with Susan Pederson and her niece. She had promised to meet Abby at the suite afterwards.

Abby saw Ned and Hans standing near the refreshment table, sampling the assortment of chips, crackers and nuts. Dr. Houston held court in the center of the room surrounded by Jeffrey, Chloe and Valerie Lendl. Abby was surprised to see Bill Briley standing in the corner of the suite talking on his cell phone.

"Hello, Abby," Valerie said, waving to her. "Come join the party."

Abby walked over to the table. "I hope I'm not late."

"Not at all," Valerie said. "The party's just getting started." She pointed to Briley. "I even brought a date with me, though it's not what he thinks. I'm determined to prove to that stubborn man that there's no way Marcus Wolfe is the thief."

"So you don't believe it either?"

Valerie shook her head. "Absolutely not. Unfortunately, all the evidence seems to be against him."

Jeffrey joined in the conversation. "You need to let it go, Valerie. Detective Briley solved the case."

"That's right," Chloe said with a smile. "We don't have to worry about any more thefts on *Antique Adventures*. Those days are over."

Abby couldn't keep silent any longer. Not when she knew the identity of the real thief. "Marcus Wolfe didn't steal my catbird painting, though someone did a very thorough job of trying to frame him for it."

"It was found in his room," Briley said, slipping his cell phone into his pocket as he walked over to join the group. "There's no doubt about it. We found the forgery he made in his room," Briley said. "He obviously copied it from the original and we'll find that one soon too."

Abby wasn't rattled by his confidence. "That forgery was planted in his room to make Marcus look guilty."

"Then who's the real thief?" Jeffrey asked.

Abby's gaze scanned the circle of people surrounding her. "Someone in this room."

"The plot thickens," Ned said ominously.

Everyone began looking at one another, uncertainty in their eyes. Abby watched them, wondering if the guilty party would try to escape before she had a chance to present all the facts. But no one moved.

"I've already cleared everyone here of suspicion," Briley announced. "I still say it has to be Wolfe. He probably forged the painting himself since he used to go to some fancy French art school."

"I've known Marcus for over a decade," Valerie said, "and he's no more of a thief than I am."

Briley arched a brow in her direction. "Then maybe I should search your room as well."

"If you do," Abby interjected, "I believe you'll find the old quilt that I wrapped around my catbird painting when I left Sparrow Island."

"What?" Valerie's blue eyes widened in shock. "That was your quilt?"

Abby nodded. "Complete with rips and stains. I'm sorry to admit that neither my sister nor I took good care of that particular family heirloom."

"So you're telling us Valerie's the thief?" Briley asked skeptically. "Does that mean I have to arrest my own date?"

"It's not Valerie," Abby assured them. "One of the maids reported today that she saw the missing quilt in Valerie's room. I just found out about it from the supervisor before coming to the party. It just reaffirmed for me who I believe the real suspect to be."

"This doesn't make any sense." Valerie sank into her chair. "I bought that quilt from an old man I met in the hotel lobby. He spun some yarn about how his mother made the quilt for him before she died. That was right before he offered to sell it to me for a ridiculous price."

"And you bought it anyway?" Jeffrey asked her.

"After we negotiated awhile." Valerie rubbed her temple. "I definitely got the better end of the deal. Of course, now I know why. It was stolen property."

"So some old man is the thief?" Hans ventured.

Dr. Houston cleared his throat. "I hope you're not accusing me."

Abby shook her head. "No, although I did wonder why you were seen arguing with a maid, especially when I suspected the thief had posed as a maid."

Dr. Houston flushed. "I thought she'd taken some money from my dresser, but I found out later I'd simply misplaced it. I assure you I apologized profusely to her for my error."

"So who is the old man?" Jeffrey asked.

"There is no old man," Abby replied.

The group considered her words and even Briley looked pensive.

"But why sell the quilt here?" Dr. Houston said at last. "Wouldn't it be better to hide the evidence of the theft and sell it at a later time and place?"

"That's what I thought too," Abby replied, "then I realized that the quilt was just a bonus. All the thief was really interested in was making a plausible reproduction of my Audubon painting."

"Which meant the thief needed supplies," Dr. Houston said, rubbing his chin, "Like the canvas and paint and the materials to age the painting so it looked authentic. None of which come cheap."

"That's why the thief sold me the quilt," Valerie mused, "to use the proceeds to finance the forgery."

"After masquerading as a hotel maid to break into Dr. Stanton's room and steal the catbird painting," Jeffrey added.

Abby appreciated the opportunity to go over the facts once more. She still didn't want to believe it, but she also didn't want Marcus to be accused of a crime he didn't commit.

"I can't stand the suspense any longer," Dr. Houston cried, "who is this master of disguise, this great artist and sneaky thief all rolled into one?"

Abby knew it was the moment of truth. She took a deep breath and said, "Chloe Cooper."

Everyone in the room turned to stare at Chloe.

Anger flashed in the young woman's blue eyes. "That is patently ridiculous."

Jeffrey shook his head. "Chloe, how could you do something like that?"

"Why do you believe her?" Chloe looked to her friend for support. "Just because she was your professor ages ago? She obviously wasn't a very good one if you're stuck working as a production assistant."

"She was a great professor," Jeffrey retorted. "And if she says you're the thief, I believe her."

Briley turned to Abby. "So where's your proof, Dr. Stanton? I thought this one had an alibi."

"So did I," Abby admitted. "When Betty claimed her teapot was stolen, I assumed the thief had struck again during a time I was actually with Jeffrey and Chloe, as well as Ned and Hans. That's why I never considered any of them as possible suspects."

"I still say the thief is someone from the San Juan Islands," Briley insisted. "Most crimes are perpetrated by someone the victim knows. It just makes sense."

"Yes, it does," Chloe exclaimed. "Certainly more sense than accusing me!"

"I've worked with this young woman for almost four years now," Dr. Houston said. He looked at Abby, confusion marring his brow. "Perhaps you'd be good enough to explain to us why you believe she's the thief."

Abby gathered her thoughts, knowing how long it had taken her to weave the tiny threads together into an unmistakable pattern.

"The first clue was an obvious one," she began. "Chloe was given my hotel room number during the preliminary evaluation of the catbird painting. I even saw her write it down on the clipboard."

"Along with hundreds of other room numbers," Chloe scoffed.

Jeffrey raised his hand to speak. "In all fairness, I knew your room number too. We don't try to hide them. Anyone on the crew could have easily seen it."

"But how many of them saw Dr. Houston's reaction when he looked at the painting?" She turned to the appraiser. "I'm sorry to say that you don't have a very good poker face, Dr. Houston. I'd just met you, so I couldn't be certain what your reaction meant, but Chloe's been working with you for quite a while now. I'm sure she knew exactly what you were thinking."

"So now I'm a mind reader too?" Chloe bit out. "This is completely bogus."

"What else convinced you?" Valerie asked Abby, leaning forward in her chair.

"That same Monday, Chloe overheard me tell Jeffrey that my sister and I were meeting the rest of our Sparrow Island friends for dinner." Abby could see the panic growing on Chloe's face. "So she knew no one would be in our room."

"That doesn't prove anything," Chloe muttered.

Now that she'd been caught, the woman wasn't a good actress. Guilt radiated from her.

"I had dessert backstage with Jeffrey and his friends on Tuesday afternoon," Abby continued. "I haven't seen Chloe again until tonight. According to Jeffrey, she had a bad head cold."

"That's right," Dr. Houston said, "We were short-handed

both yesterday and today with Chloe being sick. She seems to contract viruses very easily. Weak immune system."

Abby took a deep breath. "I think she used illness as an excuse to stay in her room and paint the forgery. As soon as she spoke tonight, I knew she hadn't been sick. In fact, there's no sign at all that she's been suffering from a head cold."

Every eye turned once again to Chloe as Abby continued making her case.

"She doesn't have a red nose or puffy, watery eyes. No sneezing or sniffles, and I haven't heard her cough once. Most people still have some degree of cold symptoms for a least a week after the worst of it is over."

Jeffrey slowly nodded as he stared a Chloe. "You could barely talk last night when you called to tell me you were still too sick to work today. And now you seem miraculously better."

"I ate a lot of chicken soup," Chloe retorted, then she whirled on Abby. "If this is your idea of proof, then I don't think I have anything to worry about. The police will laugh you right out of the station if you try to accuse me of this crime."

"You're right," Abby agreed. "All the facts I just stated are purely circumstantial. Except for the red paint staining your cuticles."

Chloe looked down at her hands and blanched, curling her fingers to hide them from sight.

"I first noticed it on Tuesday, which was after my painting was stolen. I thought it was simply the remains of fingernail polish. Now that I've seen the forgery, I know that it's paint. The color on your nails is an identical match to the red in the painting."

"Oil paints do leave stains like that," Dr. Houston commented, staring in disbelief at Chloe's hands. "It gets absorbed into the nail bed and cuticles, so even baby oil and paint thinner won't get it all off."

Briley hitched up his pants. "I bet the crime lab can match the paint on her fingernails with the paint on that forgery." He met Chloe's gaze. "That will be all the evidence the police need to make an arrest."

Chloe started backing away from the group. "I won't allow it."

Jeffrey turned to her. "You can't beat this, Chloe. It would be better if you just confessed."

"Confess?" She shook her head. "No. Never."

Dr. Houston rose gingerly to his feet, his body creaking with age. "Anyone talented enough to almost fool me into believing her painting was an original Audubon should also be smart enough to know when the jig is up."

Chloe looked frantically around the room, finally realizing that no one believed her. Then she turned on her heel and bolted for the door.

When she opened it, Mary sat in her wheelchair on the other side, her fist raised to knock on the door of the suite. As soon as Finnegan saw Chloe, the golden fur stood up on the back of his neck and he growled low as he moved protectively in front of Mary.

"Looks like the eyewitness has made a positive identification of the thief," Briley said, rising to his feet. "Chloe Cooper, I'm placing you under a citizen's arrest until the police arrive."

"Eyewitness?" Jeffrey echoed. "What does that mean?"

"Finnegan was shoved into a dark closet during the theft," Abby explained. "His reaction to Chloe proves that she's the one who did it. I've never seen him act this way with anyone before."

Mary rolled her wheelchair into the doorway, fully blocking

the exit. Then she gave the dog a command. Finnegan sat down, though he still kept a wary eye on his nemesis.

Chloe backed away from the door, defeat in her eyes. "This isn't fair," she cried out. "This just isn't fair."

"So you really did do it," Jeffrey said, as if he hadn't fully believed it until that moment. "You've been stealing antique paintings and putting forgeries in their place all this time?"

"Yes, I did it," Chloe finally admitted. Her face twisted with anger. "The producers told me three years ago that I was next in line for Houston's job. They were just waiting for him to announce his retirement or—"

"Kick the bucket?" Dr. Houston asked defiantly. "I'm not quite ready to leave this mortal plane yet."

"You don't understand. I was counting on that promotion." Chloe tipped up her chin. "My salary would have tripled. But one year passed, then two, and Dr. Houston was still here."

"Sorry to disappoint you," he said dryly. Despite his acerbic words there was a sadness clouding his eyes.

"Is that why you started stealing?" Jeffrey asked her. "To sell off the real thing and generate some cash?"

"The cash was a bonus," Chloe explained. "But I mainly needed a way to make Dr. Houston believe he wasn't up to the job anymore so he'd finally retire or get fired."

"All those mistakes I thought I made," Dr. Houston breathed, staring at Chloe. "They weren't mistakes at all, were they? You replaced the real thing with forgeries, just like you did with the catbird painting."

"That's right." Chloe affirmed. "And most of the time you didn't discover your mistake until another appraiser pointed it out." A proud smile curved her mouth. "I tricked one of the best in the business."

Dr. Houston turned away from her, distaste on his face. "I think the only one you tricked was yourself in thinking you could get away with it."

Briley grasped Chloe by her arm. "Come on, Cooper, let's go. The police will want to talk to you."

"You can't do this to me," Chloe cried as he pulled her toward the door. "I have a master's degree. I have major artistic talent. I deserve more than this."

"That's enough," Briley commanded, then he turned to Abby with a new respect in his eyes. "Congratulations, Dr. Stanton. You solved the case."

Chloe's shoulders sagged at his words. She walked out of the room with the former police detective, making a very wide berth around the watchful Finnegan.

"Wow," Ned exclaimed when they were gone. "That was really something.

Abby turned to the group. "I'm sorry this had to happen. I know this ordeal hasn't been easy for any of you."

"It's not your fault," Jeffrey told her. "I'm just glad we finally know the truth. Friends don't lie to each other and she's been deceiving all of us for much too long."

The party lasted late into the evening, finally breaking up when Dr. Houston announced he wouldn't be retiring after all. Abby left with her sister, feeling exhausted after the events of the day. For the first time since she'd arrived in Seattle she was finally ready to go home.

CHAPTER ❦ TWENTY-FIVE

THE NEXT MORNING, ABBY and her sister waited in line near the front desk of the hotel. After Chloe's arrest, the police had searched her hotel room and found the real painting hidden there, much to Abby's relief.

Now Abby held the Audubon painting in her arms, wrapped in the old quilt that Valerie had returned to her.

"I can't believe our vacation is almost over," Mary told her sister. "It seems like we just got here, yet so much has happened to both of us."

Abby certainly hadn't imagined such a trip when she'd booked their reservations a month ago. "Did you have a good time?"

Mary grinned. "Eventually. It's a vacation I'll never forget, I can tell you that."

"Me neither." Abby still hadn't seen Marcus, though Briley had assured her he'd been released as soon as the police recorded Chloe's confession.

The hotel clerk smiled at them when they reached the front of the line. "Checking out today, ladies?"

"Yes, we are," Abby told him. "May we leave our bags here while we go eat breakfast?"

"Certainly," he replied, taking their plastic key cards. "I hope you didn't have any problems during your stay at the Bristol."

Mary and Abby exchanged glances. Then Mary turned to him and said, "None that we couldn't solve."

After they finished checking out, Abby and Mary headed for the restaurant.

"Why don't we eat breakfast in the courtyard?" Mary suggested. "Finnegan has hardly been outdoors all week and I want him to enjoy himself before we take that boat ride. He's not getting any more of that awful medicine this time around."

"That sounds like a fine place for breakfast," Abby said, turning past the restaurant and heading toward the French doors that led to the courtyard. She opened them to let Mary and Finnegan through, then followed them outside.

"For Abby's a jolly smart lady, for Abby's a jolly smart lady . . ."

She looked up in surprise to see all her Sparrow Island friends seated at one of the tables. After everything that had happened, she'd been a little wary about seeing them again, aware their feelings still might be a little raw from the events that had occurred during the last week. But this breakfast surprise party put all those fears to rest.

"For Abby's a jolly smart lady, that nobody can deny . . ."

Abby laughed at their variation of the song as Mary began to sing along. Her heart warmed at the camaraderie she heard in their voices.

"Thank you," she said, applauding when they'd finished. "You don't know how much that means to me."

"We're just glad you got your catbird painting back," Thelma told her. "What you and Mary went through with that woman breaking into your room was just awful."

"What some of you went through was awful too," Abby replied, taking a seat at the table. "And I'm truly sorry for that. I hope there aren't any hard feelings."

"Do we have to sing again to prove to you that there aren't any?" Joe asked. "In case you didn't notice, Abby, I can't carry a tune."

"I noticed," Lindsey teased, then turned to Abby. "Please, don't make him sing it again."

Abby laughed, her heart lighter than it had been in days. "Okay, I won't make Joe sing. I also won't ever forget this vacation because all of you made it so very special."

A shadow fell over the table and everyone fell silent as Betty approached them. "I'm sorry to interrupt, but I just wanted to say good-bye."

Thelma stiffened in her chair, her back to her sister.

"You don't have to talk to me, Thelma," Betty said when her sister made no reply. "But I've been sitting in my room thinking about everything we've been through together, all the way back to when we were little girls. That's when I decided I didn't want it to end like this."

Thelma's lips quivered, but she pressed them together, her back ramrod straight.

Betty faltered for a moment, then lifted her chin and continued. "I just wanted to tell you again that I'm sorry, Thelma. I'm sorry I lied to you. Pride made me sell Mama's teapot instead of asking for help. Pride almost made me leave Seattle today without seeing you again."

A small sound emanated from Thelma's throat and Abby saw her swallow hard.

"I know I don't deserve your forgiveness," Betty said softly. "I've hurt you too much. I just want you to know that I love you and that you'll always be my big sister."

Thelma crumpled at those words. She turned around and threw herself in Betty's arms. "I love you too. I always have. And of course, I forgive you. If I forgave you for breaking my nose with that baseball when I was nine, I can forgive you for anything."

The sisters clung to each other, their sobs mingling with their laughter.

"Thank You, God," Abby whispered.

Mary reached over and clasped Abby's hand, tears shining in her eyes. "Amen."

When breakfast arrived, Betty joined the group and they talked and laughed together as they dined on muffins and fresh fruit.

"Now that we've reconciled," Thelma told her sister, "something tells me we're going to be closer than ever. It took us ten years to find each other again, so we have a lot of catching up to do."

"I can't wait," Betty replied, splitting a poppy seed muffin in two and setting one half on Thelma's plate.

Abby picked up her hot tea, inhaling a hint of lemon. The September sun peeked out from behind a cloud, signaling a bright day ahead.

The beautiful day was made even more so because of the

happy reunion that had happened right in front of her. She was so glad that Thelma had finally realized a sister was much more important than a teapot.

LATER THAT MORNING they all boarded the *Victoria Clipper* for their journey back to Sparrow Island.

"This vacation isn't over yet," Hugo reminded them. "We'll be taking the scenic tour back to Sparrow Island and sailing by Victoria and the spectacular views of the Olympic and Cascade mountain ranges."

Everyone began talking at once and Abby took that moment to say a silent prayer of thanksgiving to God for all the blessings He'd given her.

"Now that our trip is winding down," Thelma said, pulling her notebook out of her bag, "I need to finish my newspaper article."

Everyone groaned.

"None of that now," she admonished. "I need a quote from each one of you about what you enjoyed most on the trip."

"The great restaurants," Hugo said, before anyone could beat him to it.

"Room service," Lindsey said with a grin. "And the chance to sleep late in the mornings without anyone calling me about a horse emergency."

The group laughed as Thelma turned to Joe. "How about you, Joe?"

"Well," he said with a sheepish smile, "I have a confession to make."

"What's that?" Hugo asked him.

"Instead of having my baseball evaluated," Joe confided to

them, "I skipped out to watch the second game of the Yankees and Mariners doubleheader. The first one sounded so good on the radio that I didn't want to miss it."

Abby smiled at Joe, realizing that knowing his secret only made her admire him more. He hadn't let that one stumble in his youth hold him back or deter him from his dreams. He'd used it to strengthen his character and guide him in the right direction.

"It's hard to narrow this vacation down to just one thing," Hugo mused. "In addition to the great restaurants, I also liked the people-watching."

"I liked looking at all those antiques," added Naomi.

"Slow down," Thelma said, scribbling furiously in her notebook, "or I'm going to get it all mixed up."

"I don't think that matters," Mary told her. "We all shared in it together—the good and the bad."

As the group began to disperse, Abby turned to the windows to watch the passing scenery. That's when she saw Marcus standing on the outer deck.

She knew it was finally time to face him.

"May I join you?"

Marcus turned around, then smiled at Abby. "Of course."

Relief flowed through her that he wasn't angry. Which was somewhat surprising given that he'd been accused of stealing her catbird painting and hauled down to the police station for questioning.

"How are you?" she asked, slipping her hands over the rail. The coolness of the metal felt good on her palms. "I called your hotel room a few times last night, but you didn't answer."

"Mr. Briley took me out for dinner as an apology for all my trouble," Marcus explained. "Once that man starts talking, he doesn't stop. I know more about criminal procedure than I ever thought possible."

Abby smiled. "Then you aren't upset with me?"

His eyes widened. "Why ever would I be?"

She hesitated for a moment, then continued. "If you and I hadn't spent so much time together, Mr. Briley probably wouldn't have suspected you and Chloe wouldn't have gotten the idea to frame you for the theft. I'm sorry you got dragged into this mess, Marcus."

He stared out at the water. "It was nothing more than I deserved."

She stared at him, wondering how he could think such a thing. "No one deserves what you went through."

He sighed. "Don't be so sure. I have a confession to make." He turned to face her. "I was almost certain your bird painting was an Audubon as soon as I saw it. I've spent enough time in the art world to recognize the real thing. That's why I made an offer on it."

"I thought it was an Audubon too," Abby replied with a smile. "That's why I turned you down."

He chuckled. "Seems we both have good taste."

"I guess so."

Marcus took a step closer to her, growing more serious now. "I'd like to see you again, Abby. This week has been very special for me."

Abby saw Hugo out of the corner of her eye and knew what her answer had to be. "I'd be honored to call you my friend."

He tilted his head to one side. "Friend?"

"I'm afraid that's all I can give you, Marcus."

He nodded. "I won't say I'm not disappointed, but I'm old enough to know that some things are simply not meant to be."

She breathed a sigh of relief that he wasn't going to push the matter. Abby liked Marcus, but her heart could never belong to him.

However, she did have something else to give him. "Will you wait here for a moment?"

"Sure," he said, as she hurried back to the lower deck.

A few minutes later, she returned holding a package in her arms. "I have a gift for you."

His eyes widened. "What's the occasion?"

"Let's call it a thank you gift. I had a wonderful time in Seattle and a big part of that was due to meeting you."

He smiled. "I'm glad."

"Here," she said, pulling the old quilt he'd admired out of the box. "I want you to have this."

His mouth fell open. "Abby! I don't know what to say."

She relished his reaction, knowing he truly appreciated the gift. "Say you'll take better care of it than I have. It's been in a garage for as long as I can remember. It deserves much better care than that."

He hugged the folded quilt to his chest. "I'll treasure it."

"I know you will," she said softly.

"Have you decided what to do with the Audubon?"

That question had been on her mind since she'd learned of its authenticity. She'd prayed about it and finally come to a decision that gave her peace. "I'm donating it to the Sparrow Island Nature Conservatory."

"Abby, are you sure? It's quite valuable."

"Yes, I'm sure," she said without hesitation. "The conservatory has given me so much—a wonderful job that I love and the opportunity to live near my family again. I want to give something back."

His face softened as he looked at her. "I don't think you realize how much you give in return."

She smiled at the compliment. "Thank you, Marcus. That means a lot to me."

He picked up her hand, giving it a warm squeeze. "Au revoir, Abby."

"Good-bye."

She watched him turn around and walk to the upper deck, disappearing inside. She hoped she hadn't seen the last of Marcus Wolfe. This vacation had already given her so much.

Including a new friend.

CHAPTER ❧ TWENTY-SIX

On SATURDAY AFTERNOON, Abby returned to her laboratory at the conservatory, refreshed and renewed. She couldn't wait to get back to work, feeling as if she'd been gone much too long.

"How's our patient?" Abby asked Bobby McDonald. She bent down next to the owlet's cage to get a closer look at the little orphan.

"He's awesome," Bobby told her. "He's getting bigger every day and flapping his wings all the time. You should see him eat! He even pounced on a cricket that hopped into his cage yesterday morning."

Abby was glad to hear it. She knew they had to release the owlet before he became too domesticated and lost his hunting instincts. It wouldn't be easy for him to survive in the wild on his own at such a young age, but the owlet had youth and vivacity on his side.

He was just like her Grandma Lora, who didn't have much more than that during her foray into the world on the orphan train. She'd not only survived, but thrived. Abby remembered her grandma humming old hymns as she worked and how she'd always said that every day was a blessing from God.

Abby sometimes thought that she had been given so much in her own life that she didn't always appreciate God's daily gifts. She paused in her work for a moment to watch Bobby as he talked to the owlet. She had such wonderful friends and neighbors, a job that she loved, a nice house to live in and plenty of food and clothing. She had more than so many people in the world.

Best of all, she had her faith to sustain her through good times and bad, like her parents and grandparents and great-grandparents had before her. A great cloud of witnesses who had faced the trials in life and leaned on each other and their God to see them through.

She smiled, recalling one of her mother's favorite Bible verses.

"Therefore, since we are surrounded by such a great cloud of witnesses, let us throw off everything that hinders and the sin that so easily entangles, and let us run with perseverance the race marked out for us" (Hebrews 12:1).

The door to the lab opened, breaking Abby's reverie, and Hugo walked inside. He often worked on Saturday since so many tourists came through the conservatory on the weekend.

"How's Fred?" he asked, using the name Bobby had given the owlet.

"He's almost ready to leave the nest," Abby told him. "Have a look for yourself."

Hugo leaned down near the cage, then smiled as the owlet blinked solemnly at him. "He looks good. Have you set a release date yet?"

"I'm thinking sometime next week." She turned to Bobby. "You'd better scoot if you want to get home in time to go on that picnic your parents have planned this afternoon."

"Thanks for reminding me," Bobby said, grabbing his backpack off the counter. "Bye, Mr. Baron. Bye, Abby. Bye, Fred." Then he was out the door.

Hugo chuckled. "I really like that boy."

"So do I." Abby looked around the lab, knowing she couldn't start any new projects until Monday. Yet, she wasn't quite ready to leave.

"Have you had a chance to tell your mother about the locket?" Hugo asked.

"Mary and I stopped by the farm earlier today." Abby turned to face him. "It was hard for my sister to reveal the secret Grandma Lora had told her so many years ago, but my mother understood."

"I knew she would." Hugo was a good friend of both George and Ellen Stanton. "And the locket?

Abby glanced up at him with a smile. "I have to admit I was a little apprehensive about telling her it had been looted after the fire. She was stunned."

"I can imagine."

She swallowed a sigh. "I guess we'll never know if Grandma Lora was one of the looters or how she got the locket."

"Does that bother Ellen?"

Abby shook her head. "No, she's just so grateful that we learned something about that time in her mother's life and now know more about the locket's origins. And the fact that it's her grandmother's lock of hair inside the locket, when she's wondered about it her entire life, really meant a lot to her."

"I'm glad to hear it. Sometimes we gain a deeper understanding of our loved ones," Hugo said, "when we learn about the mistakes they made and the challenges they faced."

Abby agreed with him. Her own mistakes had taught her so much through the years, even more so than the acclaim she'd garnered for her work. Then she thought about her sister and the challenges she faced every day since becoming disabled. She admired Mary now more than she ever had.

"I wonder what Chloe Cooper will learn from her mistakes," Hugo said. "Have you heard anything more about her?"

"I received an e-mail from Mr. Briley this morning. She's made a full confession, though she doesn't regret her actions. Not yet, anyway. She feels a sense of entitlement for all the things she was denied in her life."

"Denied?" Hugo shook his head. "She was given the means and ability to achieve a master's degree, the talent to paint something as beautiful as that gray catbird, and yet she feels cheated. Amazing."

Abby shared his disbelief. "I hope she'll come to see the truth someday. It's like that song the children sing in Sunday school. Count your blessings every day and you'll see all the good things God has done." She smiled up at him. "I'm paraphrasing, of course."

He smiled back at her. "It's humbling, isn't it, to actually count our blessings? I have so many to be thankful for."

"So do I," Abby said, knowing the man standing beside her

was one of them. A good friend. A great boss. A man who had brought so much to Sparrow Island when he'd built the conservatory and The Nature Museum.

"I want to thank you again for donating the Audubon painting to the conservatory," he said. "It's a perfect fit, since our mission is to cherish and celebrate nature and wildlife."

"It was my pleasure," Abby declared, feeling a weight of relief lift from her shoulders. Sometimes the blessings in life came with responsibility and Abby knew she'd made the right decision.

The catbird had found a new home.

CHAPTER ❦ TWENTY-SEVEN

ONE MONTH LATER

Abby walked out of Little Flock church on Sunday morning, uplifted by Rev. Hale's message that behind every challenge in life might be a blessing in disguise.

She met her sister on the lawn, where Mary was visiting with friends. Both of them liked to linger outside after the service. It was one of Abby's favorite times of the week, a chance to share in fellowship.

Ellen Stanton approached her daughters. "There you two are. I was hoping you hadn't left yet."

"Where's Dad?" Abby asked, leaning over to give her mother a hug.

"He and Sam just took off in Sam's truck to go fishing. They've been looking forward to it all week."

George Stanton loved to fish. He'd passed on that same passion for the sport to Sam.

"It'll be just us girls for dinner today," Ellen said, her blue eyes twinkling. "It will be just us girls, and I have something I want to share with you."

"What?" Mary asked.

Ellen smiled. "It's a surprise."

Abby was intrigued. She and Mary enjoyed eating Sunday dinner with their parents, who usually invited other guests as well. She couldn't remember the last time just the three of them had spent Sunday afternoon together. "I hope the surprise is your roast chicken and sweet potato pie for dessert."

Ellen was a wonderful cook and Abby knew that whatever she had planned for dinner would be delicious.

Twenty minutes later, they were at Stanton Farm, the three of them seated around the table in the warm, cozy kitchen. The chicken roasting in the oven gave off a savory aroma that made Abby's mouth water. She could hardly wait until it was time to eat.

"So what's the surprise?" Mary asked, Finnegan asleep at her feet. "Is it the roast chicken or something even better?"

"Something better," Ellen replied as she got up and retrieved a thick envelope from the kitchen counter. "Something amazing."

Mary and Abby exchanged glances, neither one of them having a clue.

"I received a letter yesterday," Ellen told them, "from a woman in Missouri." She pulled a two-page letter from the padded envelope. "Her name is Olivia Foster."

Abby turned the name over in her mind, but it didn't ring a bell. "I don't think I know her."

"Just listen," Ellen said softly. She laid the letter on the table and gently smoothed the creases out with her fingers.

"Dear Mrs. Stanton," Ellen began. *"You don't know me, but I'm an avid fan of the television show* Antique Adventures *and I saw your daughter present an antique gold locket on the show last week. You can't imagine my shock when I heard the story behind it. You see, Mrs. Stanton, your mother's story is my aunt's story too."*

"Her aunt?" Mary echoed. "I don't understand."

"You will," Ellen promised, then she continued reading.

"Ninety-five years ago, my eleven-year-old aunt boarded an orphan train in New York City bound for the Midwest. She talked about that trip often, as well as the hard life she'd had prior to her journey. Her parents had died when she was very young and she'd been raised on the streets by her older brother. Some of the stories she told me were quite harrowing, and I'm still surprised she survived. But there came a time when her brother could no longer care for her. That's when he made the painful decision to put her on the orphan train so she could find a new family."

"That poor girl," Mary murmured. "And her poor brother."

Abby's heart ached for the two of them, desperate to survive and stay together. Even worse, she knew there had been thousands of others like them. Children struggling on their own during a time when there weren't many safety nets available for them.

"You're probably wondering by now," Ellen read, *"what my aunt's story has to do with the segment I saw on television. Well, she met a girl on that train by the name of Lora Deal."*

Mary gasped. "Grandma!"

Ellen nodded, her face wreathed in a smile. "Yes, Mary. This woman's aunt knew my mother."

"Keep reading," Abby encouraged, wanting to hear the rest of the story. Her heart pounded in her chest. This letter might contain some of the answers they'd been seeking for so long.

Ellen turned her attention back to the letter.

"Lora and my aunt became instant friends. They discovered that they shared the same birthday and soon thought of themselves as sisters. We can only imagine how painful it must have been for them to know they had to part again after just meeting. My aunt said they often talked about it and promised to try and find each other after they were adopted."

Abby had forgotten all about the roast chicken in the oven or her hunger. Her entire focus was on the story of two eleven-year-old girls on a long, fateful train ride.

"When they reached the Midwest, the train began to stop in each town for the children to be adopted. Both my aunt and Lora knew that they could be separated at any time. Desperate to have something to remember each other by, they decided to exchange gifts. Neither one of them owned much, but my aunt had a locket that her brother had given to her before she'd left on the orphan train."

Abby sat back in her chair, amazed at the sudden revelation. The locket had been given to Grandma Lora by her friend. Later, Grandma Lora must have put her mother's hair in it. That's why it had been so special to her.

"My aunt didn't know where her brother got the locket," Ellen continued, *"and had learned during her years living on the street not to ask such questions. All I know is that he gave his little sister something of great value, knowing he wouldn't be around to care for her anymore."*

"A gift of love," Mary whispered.

Abby leaned forward, waiting to hear the rest. When her mother turned to the second page, she felt a pang of disappointment, realizing this wondrous story was almost over.

"She gave Lora her most prized possession, and Lora did the same. The next day, my aunt was adopted by a family in Iowa. She never saw or heard from Lora again, despite all of her efforts to find her."

A tear trickled down Ellen's cheek. She didn't bother to wipe it away, but kept reading, her voice quavering now.

"My aunt never forgot her friend Lora, whom she called her sister in spirit. She even named her first daughter after her. I just want you and your family to know how thrilled we were to finally see the locket that we'd heard so much about and thought you'd like to know how it came into your mother's possession."

"What was her aunt's name?" Mary asked softly.

Ellen met her oldest daughter's gaze. "Her name was Ellen. They named their daughters after each other."

Tears of joy welled in Abby's eyes. "What a wonderful way for the two of them to honor each other. They must have formed such a strong bond in the short time they were together on the orphan train."

Mary wiped a tear from her cheek. "Does the letter say what Grandma Lora gave to her friend? What was her most precious possession?"

Ellen reached into the padded envelope and pulled out a slim journal. "It was her diary."

Abby's mouth dropped open as she stared at the faded red cover. When her mother opened it, she saw pages and pages filled with the neat, precise script that her grandmother had always possessed.

"It's been so long since I lost her." Ellen's voice broke with tears of happiness. "I feel like I've been given the gift of my mother again after all these years."

"Have you read it?" Mary asked, her voice barely a whisper.

"Twice," Ellen said, then gave a watery laugh. "I was up half the night. The journal is filled with details of my mother's life before she rode the orphan train. All of her hopes and dreams and fears. I read it so fast, I didn't even comprehend it all. That's why I'd like to read it again this afternoon with the two of you."

"I can't think of anything else I'd rather do," Abby said honestly.

The oven timer went off and Ellen got up to take out the roast chicken. The grease in the hot enamel pan sputtered as she placed it on top of the stove.

"Can we read just one passage before we eat?" Mary implored.

Ellen gave her an indulgent smile. "Well, we should wait a few minutes before we carve the chicken. And I know the perfect passage to read to you. It's the very last entry in her diary."

Ellen sat down at the table and picked up the journal, carefully handling it like the treasure it was. Then she turned to the back and cleared her throat.

"Almost half the other children are gone now and I know Ellen or I could be next. We're both scared, but we've been praying together and know that God will keep us safe. Ellen told me she never prayed before she met me, but when I told her about Jesus and how God's love is forever, she said she wanted to be part of His family."

Ellen turned the page.

"I don't want to leave her, but I know we'll see each other again. I recited a Bible verse from John 14:2 that my father used to read to me before he died.

"*'In my Father's house are many rooms; if it were not so, I would have told you. I am going there to prepare a place for you.'*

"*When I am lonely or scared, I remember that someday I will be together again with the people I love in my Father's house.*

"*My dearest Ellen, I hope this diary gives you comfort. I know we'll meet again someday because the Bible tells us so. Remember that I will always love you.*"

No one broke the silence when Ellen finished reading. Grandma Lora might have been writing it for her friend, but her message resonated with all of them.

"It almost seems as if she wrote those last lines just for me," Ellen said softly. "I feel such peace each time I read them."

The words comforted Abby too. The secret of the locket had finally been revealed. Love never died, it just flowed from generation to generation, growing with each new heart it touched.

Like the fine links in the locket's gold chain, that love connected each one of them to the past and to the future. Forever and ever, amen.

A NOTE FROM THE EDITORS

THIS ORIGINAL BOOK WAS created by the Books and Inspirational Media Division of Guideposts, the world's leading inspirational publisher. Founded in 1945 by Dr. Norman Vincent Peale and his wife Ruth Stafford Peale, Guideposts helps people from all walks of life achieve their maximum personal and spiritual potential. Guideposts is committed to communicating positive, faith-filled principles for people everywhere to use in successful daily living.

Our publications include award-winning magazines like *Guideposts*, *Angels on Earth* and *Positive Thinking*, best-selling books, and outreach services that demonstrate what can happen when faith and positive thinking are applied in day-to-day life.

For more information, visit us online at www.guideposts.org, call (800) 431-2344 or write Guideposts, 39 Seminary Hill Road, Carmel, New York 10512.